INITIATION

At another signal from Sheelah, the Moon lifted the sheets from the figure on the litter. The Moon stripped off all Jenny's clothes, leaving only the bandage on her eyes. She looked down with bitter envy at the smooth, pearl-white body.

The room was full of aromatic, dizzying smoke from the incense dish. There was no sound except the sizzle of burning incense.

With the Moon's help, Sheelah anointed the girl's body. All the time she worked, Sheelah intoned invocations to the demons in a small, high voice. Sheelah had never failed; but Sheelah had never used her skills on a sophisticated, highly educated, tough-minded Anglo-Saxon woman—a woman brought up to independence of spirit, with years of quick decision and violent action behind her and an inbuilt refusal to accept subjugation or defeat. . . .

THE
NECKLACE
OF SKULLS

Ivor Drummond

A DELL BOOK

Published by
Dell Publishing Co., Inc.
1 Dag Hammarskjold Plaza
New York, New York 10017

Dell ® TM 681510, Dell Publishing Co., Inc.

ISBN: 0-440-16378-1

Reprinted by arrangement with St. Martin's Press, Inc.

Printed in the United States of America

First Dell printing—March 1980

Prologue

A religious sect with fanatical adherents in all parts of India has devoutly believed, over many centuries, this account of its origin:

When the world was young, the face of the world was plagued by a demon of such awesome stature that the deepest ocean rose only to his knees. It was this demon's pleasure to devour mankind as soon as men were created by the Great Ones. It naturally fell to the goddess Kali to eliminate the demon—Kali the Destroyer, the Mother of Sorrows, the Drinker of Blood, who is sometimes black and blood-daubed, sometimes a tigress, sometimes hewn twelve-armed. Kali assailed the demon with her sword: but, as she shed its blood, each drop turned into another demon. Kali thereupon wiped the sweat from her forearm, and with it made two men. She tore strips, white and yellow, from the hem of her garment, and gave the strips to the men she had made, commanding them to strangle the new-born demons. They did so faithfully, thus enabling Kali to slay the parent demon and save mankind. In gratitude Kali gave them the strips of stuff, for themselves and their descendants for ever, at the same time laying on them a dreadful and bloody charge.

Subject to certain strict rules, and obedient to her instructions in the form of omens, they were to kill, by strangling, as many men as possible, and rob the bodies. And so they did. To a small extent this was for their gain, their livelihood. To a major extent it was an immutable religious duty, an act of worship.

In early days the goddess Kali ate the bodies of those slaughtered in her honour, which conveniently disposed of the corpses. But she strictly charged her servants that they should on no account look at her while she was dining. Once a chela, a novice of the sect, looked back, like the wife of Lot, and saw the Black Mother in the act of eating a new-killed victim. Kali refused thereafter to consume the bodies, but, in her mercy, gave to her followers one of her teeth, which they were to use as a pickaxe for digging the graves. And so they have done.

By and by the rest of India became aware that in its midst lived secretive men, false-faced, who killed and robbed on a terrifying scale. Such a man was called in Sanskrit *sthaga,* cheat. Hence came a word common to nearly all modern Indian vernaculars, *t'hag,* one who deceives, one who operates in disguise. It is generally rendered *Thug*.

The Thug spread all over India. Membership was strictly hereditary. They survived and flourished because of their secrecy, their skill in disguises, their treacherous affability; they communicated to each other in a private language; they infiltrated army, police and government, often reaching high rank, which gave them excellent intelligence.

In the early 19th century the British government of India at last took stern action against the Thugs. After protracted and brilliant police work, 1,562 were arrested, of whom 382 were hanged and 986 deported or imprisoned for life. The women and young children were condemned to celibacy, so that Thuggee would die completely.

It was believed that the Thugs were extinct. India drew a great sigh of relief.

But a wise man said, "It is never safe to assert that any ancient practice in India has been entirely suppressed."

One

Lady Jennifer Norrington sat waiting in the fast-gathering darkness.

She was hot, uncomfortable, angry and a little frightened. She was sitting on a low mud wall. Behind her stretched the huge plain of the Ganges. In front of her was a bus-stop at the edge of a West Bengal village, a huddle of mud houses full of people, cattle, images of gods, Communist slogans, and overpowering smells from the cooking-pots.

The bus was supposed to arrive at nightfall. It was not expected to be punctual. On the bus would be a group of men. They would look like ordinary poor travellers, peasant farmers, Bengali jute-growers. They would have baggage and bundles of various kinds, which would contain stolen antibiotics worth $100,000. They would transfer themselves and their bundles to bullock-carts, and disappear into the illimitable darkness of the Indian night. Unless they were stopped.

There would probably be four or five men; there might be eight or ten. They would probably not be armed, at least with guns. This was uncertain. They were probably not tough, nor used to fighting, nor trained in combat. This was also uncertain. Nothing was certain, least of all the outcome.

Jenny wished violently that someone else was doing

this job, instead of herself and two friends. It was
not her problem. She had been dragged into it. She
wanted out. She knew that if the antibiotics went off
in the bullock-carts they would reappear, in time, on
the black market. They would be diluted and hideously overpriced; they would be adulterated and
therefore dangerous. Children treated with them
could be blinded, go mad, die. She knew also that
the police could not be informed, could not help,
must never hear about any of this. She still bitterly
resented being caught up in it. She resented the bore-
dom of the long hot wait, while steaming day turned
into steaming night. She was uncomfortable on the
low wall. She disliked the possibility that an armed,
effective gang of ten men might be carrying the stolen
antibiotics.

The three of them had allies in the village, it was
true. Jenny had not seen them but she knew they were
there. It was not at all clear *why* they were there.
They could do no good. The point had been made,
most clearly, that their well-wishers were men of peace,
utterly opposed, like Gandhi himself, to violence even
in the best of causes. There were Hindus who fought,
fine soldiers, men of the warrior castes. There were
Hindus who under no provocation would raise a hand
to fight. It seemed that their allies were of the gentle,
fatalistic kind. Perhaps, thought Jenny, they were
almost saints. But she did not want soft-spoken saints
at her side, not this evening. She wanted men with
clubs and knives and loud voices.

Ishur Ghose was there too, hidden with the others
somewhere in the shadowed edge of the village. He
was a soldier. He had fought very many battles. And
his battles had been of this kind, discreet ambushes,
adroit executions. But Ishur Ghose was very old and

frail. His pipe-stem legs needed the aid of a stick; his failing eyes needed heavy spectacles. He had fought his battles for the British Government long before the Second War. He was there as their friend, and he had brought friends of his own: but for all the use they were they might as well have stayed in Calcutta.

The minutes dragged by like hours. There was nothing for Jenny to do but sit and wait. There was no point in thinking about the future, which could be faced when it came. She thought about the past, the all-too-logical sequence of events which had brought her to this steam-bath of a place, this smelly rendezvous with a gang of coffee-coloured criminals.

It was Colly Tucker's fault.

He had come, shamefaced, to her family's enormous house in Wiltshire.

"I have to go to India," he said in his soft American voice. Older, more respected, much busier Tuckers, engaged as he was not in the active management of the Tucker commercial and industrial empire, had summoned him from his yacht in the Caribbean. They had reports of large-scale thefts from the company in Calcutta, which was the headquarters of the whole far-eastern operation. John Tucker, one of Colly's serious cousins, ran the place, and his explanations were vague and unsatisfactory.

A major scandal loomed. It was impossible to suspect John Tucker: but it was horribly possible to suspect his stepson, a spoiled and wilful youth, cradled all his life in mother-love, introduced into the Calcutta office by his mother, John's wife, by dint of sustained emotional blackmail. Young Harry thought he was entitled to the top job and the top salary. His stepfather wouldn't play favourites to that point.

The boy added resentment to greed. This much was known; the deeply embarrassing consequence was guessed.

"Publicity would be a disaster," said Colly to Jenny's family at dinner. "Thing like this could torpedo the whole operation, as well as dropping old John in the, uh, manure, which would be a shame. So the heavy brass sent for me to New York and said, "Son, tuck away that yachting cap, buy a solar topee, and go clear up the mess."

"You ought to go straight to the police," said Jenny's mother.

"Just what I'd like to do, Lady Teffont," said Colly, "but from what we hear, telling the Indian cops is not the way to keep a secret."

"I should think that's true," said Jenny's father. "Especially in a city with a Communist government."

"Any stick to beat Uncle Sam with," said Colly. "And this would make a pretty big stick."

"All the same, my dear," said Lady Teffont, "I imagine you'll want local help of some kind. This odious stepson can't be doing all this stealing all on his own, and if his partners are local people—"

"That's so, ma'am. He has to sell to somebody, for one thing. I do need local help. I was kind of relying on Sandro for that."

"Is Sandro going?" asked Jenny.

"Sure."

"Oh. Then I might come."

"It never occurred to me you wouldn't," said Colly. "That's why I came here."

"But Sandro, with all his gifts, is not precisely a local in Calcutta," said Lady Teffont.

"No," said Colly, "but he does have friends. I don't know *why* he does. Pretty creepy bunch most of them are, guys in security and counter-intelligence and stuff like that. Which is what I need. Somebody who can provide a little muscle and a lot of local knowledge, and keep his mouth shut."

"When do we leave?" asked Jenny.

"Not for a while. This thing has been going on for a year. It can go on another month. I want to do a crash course in Urdu. Sandro's doing one."

"Ah. Then if both of you speak it I needn't."

The Air India jet landed at Dum Dum. John Tucker welcomed his younger cousin with that mixture of affection and contempt with which all Colly's relations treated him. Quite apart from his wealth and his shocking idleness, he had mild green eyes, untidy mousy hair, a shambling walk and a self-deprecating manner which begged for contempt even as they called for affection.

Colly performed the introduction as coolies carried the baggage, on their heads, from the customs to the car.

Jenny saw a forceful, conventional American of fifty with stiff grey hair and sharp grey eyes. John Tucker saw an English girl whose face was insanely attractive but far from intelligent. She did not, John considered, quite attain classic beauty—her face was too round, her nose too short and tilted: and when she smiled the smile dug a single dimple in her left cheek, an asymmetry of great charm but clearly against the rules of classical perfection. Her hair was bright gold, long and untidy; her eyes were large and blue and silly. Her body, as far as it could be deduced under her cotton shirt and pants, *was* perfect. John decided that Lady Jennifer looked good enough to eat but not bright enough to talk to.

"And this," said Colly, "is Sandro Ganzarello."

John Tucker switched his gaze from the juicy but

retarded English girl to the enormous Italian. Il conte
Alessandro di Ganzarello was a King Kong, a human
mountain, ugly but impressive. The barrel of his
chest, the width of his shoulders, the muscles of his
arms, threatened to burst out of the beautiful Italian
silk of his clothes; his black hair was peppered with
silver watch-springs; his face was so deeply tanned
that he was darker than many high-caste Indians, who
are careful to stay out of the sun and stay as pale
as possible: but in the midst of the dark leather of
his face were most un-Indian eyes, eyes of startling
Nordic blue, as surprising as a honey-blond child in
the slum tenements of Calcutta.

The road into the city from the airport was hideous with deep ruts and potholes. It was jammed with
carts, the shriek of their wooden wheels and the
meaningless, automatic shouts of their drivers louder
than any traffic. Each side of the road, on swampy,
undeveloped land, were acres of squalid little huts
jammed into dense colonies like those of insects. They
were made of mud, scraps of wood, gasoline cans;
they swarmed with people. Acrid smoke billowed from
cowdung cooking-fires. Among the huts, all over the
road, all along the road into Calcutta, all over Calcutta, there were impossible, unimaginable numbers
of men, little dark underfed men in identical dirty-
white dhotis.

Jenny opened the window beside her. She shut it
again immediately. The stench from the acres of huts
was overpowering, unspeakable. The acrid smoke of
the fires, not unpleasant, was drowned in the reek
from the shallow ditches, hardly scratches in the
ground, which were all the drainage of the bustees,
the cities of huts.

Sandro had been almost everywhere, but never to
Calcutta. He said, "I never saw people, so many

people, in such misery. Not in South America, not in any part of Africa. These people are hardly alive. They cannot live so. It is impossible."

"It's possible because it's an illusion," said Colly. "Right, John?"

"That pong was no illusion," said Jenny.

"To them it is. That's how they bear it. The whole of life is a brief illusion, a kind of bad dream."

"At least it doesn't go on long, not for a child in those huts."

"No, I guess it doesn't go on long."

They drove through vast areas of docks, warehouses, aged ramshackle factories, and tall baroque houses, once grand, now sprouting lush vegetation from every cranny and crammed with poor families. The streets were packed. The sides of the roads were lined with squatting vendors of wilted vegetables and plastic combs, over whom stumbled hump-backed cows and a few buffaloes and goats. If garbage was collected at all, it was collected capriciously and seldom.

"I suppose it's interesting," said Jenny. "But I don't like it. Can we please go somewhere quite different?"

They went somewhere quite different, to the smart residential suburb of Alipur. In John Tucker's big cool house in a big shady garden they returned to civilization after an excursion through a hell worse than anything in the medieval imagination.

"The contrast is more than I can cope with," said Jenny. "I didn't make those slums. So why do I feel so guilty, having this delicious drink?"

Colly had written disingenuously to his cousin to say that he and two friends needed a vacation. They were tired after doing a few exhausting things in Morocco and Kenya and other places. They wanted to see India, a little of India. Could they use John as a start point?

"Colley *tired*?" said John's wife Eleanor.

"I get tired when I do nothing," said John. "I guess Colly's the same."

"It's not fair, the way he gets so much for doing so little."

"Oh, I don't know. I like Colly. He was a nice kid and he's pretty nice still. Never gave anybody any trouble."

Eleanor, who came from Iowa, took a sterner view of life and of human merit. She had hideously spoiled her only son, but in all the rest of the world she was intolerant of sloth and weakness. She resented Colly. She resented Jenny, when the party arrived at the big cool house in Alipur, very much indeed.

Eleanor took Jenny to be vapid, frivolous and superficial. She was not to be blamed for his misapprehension: Jenny went through life sedulously acting a part remote from the toughness of her real character and the formidable scope of her real abilities. Other people were misled as Eleanor was misled; almost all others, to the point where only Sandro and Colly, who loved her and beside whom she had fought so many battles, fully knew the cobra-quick and cobra-deadly fighting machine behind the charming and silly mask.

Eleanor assumed that Jenny would want to see the smart boutiques of the Chowringhee and admire the great green expanse of the Maidan, redolent of the Raj and furnished with splendid relics.

Jenny dutifully pressed her button nose on the windows of jewellers and dressmakers; she inspected the gigantic statue of the Queen Empress, from whose left eye dribbled, like a tear, a mess made by a perching crow.

She met the others for lunch at an opulent hotel, onto the very steps of which crawled and thrashed innumerable beggars. Some pointed at their blind eye-sockets; some gestured with the stumps of arms and legs. They were revolting, and infinitely pitiable. To give to one brought down upon the giver a swarm of others; but not to give seemed monstrous.

The others had been busy. Sandro had been on the telephone to a friend in Delhi—just such a friend as Colly had known he would have. Colly had been talking to his cousin's stepson. Sandro finished the morning with a name and address; Colly finished it with a nasty taste in his mouth.

Sandro telephoned again from the hotel. He arranged that they should meet the friend of his friend in a room above a shop in a side street.

Ishur Ghose was very old indeed: not only by the standards of India, where old age begins to rush up on the poor the moment they have attained precocious adulthood, and where the life expectancy is barely forty years, but even by European standards. Wisps of white hair floated over his narrow brown skull. He was clean-shaven. His hands were very thin, but the knuckles were misshapen with arthritis. He walked slowly, stooping, with the aid of a walking-stick of black wood with a large ivory knob. He wore a beautifully embroidered heavy silk shirt over his dhoti. His wrinkled old feet were sandalled. Gold-rimmed spectacles perched on his long nose, and he wore a modern hearing-aid of an expensive type. He looked like a retired scholar with a private income.

He said to Sandro, in English better than Sandro's, "Please convey my respectful regards, Count, to our friend in Delhi when you next speak to him. It is a city full of memories for me. I was recruited into the government service there in 1920. A different government, I need hardly say. Of course my kind of appointment did not survive independence and partition, both of which, to my mind, were disasters. This is not a view I often put to my fellow countrymen. *Your* fellow countrymen, Lady Jennifer, were the best rulers India has ever had. Or at least since the days of Akbar and his son and grandson. Do you know your Indian history? I have made a considerable study of it. It is my hobby. Indeed it is my fulltime occupation now that my active career is finished. I have explored all kinds of byways of our past. Scandalous things happened, you know. Human life was held very cheap, and so were honesty and honour. Public honesty was introduced by the British. It was a completely foreign plant, and it flourished only while they were here to foster it. People talk about exploitation, and of course great fortunes were made. The nabobs, you remember. But the British put far more into India than they took out. I am, I suppose, obliged to believe this, as I served the British until the deluge. Which we had foretold, those of us whose task it was to know what was going on behind closed doors. Our advice was ignored, owing to pressure from the urban intellectuals who called themselves the Congress party. They said they represented India, but they represented the riffraff of the big cities. You will understand that I keep all this most strictly to myself, except when I am speaking to people such as you."

"What we wanted to discuss—" began Colly.

"Have you read *Kim*?" went on Ishur Ghose, remorselessly garrulous. "In many ways it is a fanciful account of the organization in which I served, though in certain regards it is quite an accurate picture, though of course of a bygone epoch. The days of yore. I am not altogether sentimental in regretting them. Please quote me to nobody, or my head would be forfeit. Of course I am speaking metaphorically."

He paused at last and looked at Colly. His eyes were as bright as jet buttons behind his gold-rimmed spectacles. He was old and he talked too much, thought Colly, but he was a long way from being senile.

"And what, Mr Tucker," he said gently, "could you possibly be wanting with a long-retired officer of the Secret Service?"

Colly waited a moment before answering. He was wondering how much to say. By Sandro's friend, Ishur Ghose had been given a character of absolute discretion as well as devious cunning. He had been, it seemed, a loyal servant of the government as well as an effective and inventive spy. That being so, it was probably safe to tell him everything; the more he knew, the more he could help.

Colly told him everything.

Ishur Ghose smiled benignly. He said, "You had to make a judgement of my character before you decided to spill all your beans, Mr Tucker. You had to decide whether you could trust this old gasbag not to blab, and whether it was worthwhile anyway. You judged favourably, and it so happens you were quite right. That gives me confidence in your judgement. Therefore when you say this young man is stealing from his stepfather I believe you. Even though you have no proof at all. If you were right about me, the odds are you were right about him also. So we proceed on the basis that your hypothesis is correct. But I must ask for a further judgement of his character. If you lean on him, will he talk?"

"Yes," said Colly immediately. "But that's exactly what I can't do, not if we want to keep this quiet."

"Quite so, my dear fellow, but it is what you must do *after* we have made a number of other preparations. I will do a bit of snooping myself. Tell me again exactly what he has been stealing?"

"Exactly what you'd expect. Stuff with high value but low bulk. Clock movements, timing and control devices for automated machinery, drugs. I mean pharmaceuticals, not dope."

"Of course. I did not expect opium or bhang in your cousin's warehouse. Very good. What I shall sniff for is items of this kind coming onto the market from obscure sources. The drugs will be relabelled, but the labels will be locally printed and probably amateurish. Yet they will be drugs that could not be manufactured locally. It is quite easy, you see. I think the police would find the pipeline quite quickly, and trace it back—"

"To the Tucker company," said Colly. "To a member of the family."

"I fully understand the problem. It is extremely familiar to India, even to some of the leading merchant families in Bombay and Madras. What I recommend, in all humility and nervousness, is that we allow this misguided young gentleman to proceed with another operation, and catch his friends in the act."

"Why not just put the fear of God into this stepson?" asked Jenny. "Sandro's good at that. I haven't met the man, but I expect you could put the fear of God into him, darling."

"*Si,*" said Sandro. "I think."

"That is a *very* bad idea, Lady Jennifer," said Ishur Ghose. "His partners in crime will not allow him to stop. He will be threatened and he will be blackmailed. Nothing whatever will be solved, and the risk of public exposure is much increased."

"Oh," said Jenny, seeing that Ishur Ghose was right.

"You two gentlemen," said Ishur Ghose, "must find out all you can, but you must do it without arousing the faintest suspicion in our man."

"Agreed," said Colly. "While you get a lead on the other end of the pipeline. And on the night we'll chop it in the middle."

"That is exactly right."

"You're lucky in your new friend, darling," said Jenny as they drove back to Alipur.

"Yeah," said Colly. "But I feel a little funny about taking Cousin Eleanor's hospitality while I'm putting a bomb under her ewe-lamb."

"What will you do with the ewe-lamb?"

"Fly him back to New York the same night we chop his friends, I hope. Then when they sing there isn't anybody to sing about. The bunghole stopped and the scandal avoided. Then I thought we might go to Kashmir to look at this houseboat proposition the ads in the *New Yorker* talk about."

"It is most ironic," said the old man. "Of course our distinguished ancestors often knew in advance about treasure being taken across country by couriers. They made some very nice hauls. But I do not know of a case in all our history when a valuable consignment of *stolen* goods has been literally dropped into our laps."

"It is a highly satisfactory state of affairs," said his companion, who was in extreme physical contrast. He was a big, powerful man, exceptionally tall and well set up for an Indian. He was in early middle age, and had a mane of thick silvering hair. His face was strong and intellectual, with a big nose, rather heavy

mouth, tall brow, and the deep sad eyes with which
most Indians look out at a discouraging world.

The younger man went on, "You are quite right—
if the thefts had been reported to the police the crime
would have been exposed already, unless some very
heavy bribing went on. I am sure we can find out
what is going to happen, and when and where."

"I hope the omens are good."

"I feel the omens are bound to be good, when the
goddess has promised so rich an offering."

Ishur Ghose's intelligence was remarkably good. He
seemed to have an army of eyes and ears in the back
streets of Calcutta, in the bazaars and tenements,
among the beggars and shopkeepers and criminals.

He reported quite soon that he knew who was buy-
ing the merchandise, and how it reached the buyer.
The latter was a bent industrialist. The middlemen
were professional criminals, but not clever ones. The
whole thing was pretty amateurish. Only John Tucker's reluctance to shop his stepson, or even to suspect him, had prevented the whole racket being blown
up months before.

With this information Colly could act. An anonymous message reached John Tucker telling him to
stocktake meticulously at very frequent intervals.

He had this done.

After a short while $100,000 worth of antibiotics,
airfreighted from America, was reported missing from
the bonded warehouse.

Colly got a message to Ishur Ghose. Then he and
Sandro leaned on John's stepson.

The result was an eighty-mile drive, in a company
car, through dusty jute-fields, north-west of Calcutta,
to this drab little village in the gathering darkness.

* * *

"Will your European friends be there when we meet the thieves?" asked the big man with the mane of silvering hair.

"The two men, oh yes, I am sure they will. They are very rich, you know. Beautiful watches and gold cigarette-cases and pockets full of money. I know it is little compared to the merchandise, but it is all grist to the mill, as my colonel used to say."

"There is no precedent for killing *feringhi*."

"Only because, in the days of our greatness—in the *other* days of our greatness—there were few *feringhi* to kill, and those few travelled well guarded and well armed. These men are not musicians or potters or mahouts or religious mendicants. They do not fall into any of the forbidden categories. The Italian is a landowner and the American is a kind of merchant."

"We can kill landowners and merchants."

"*Can?* We *must*, if the omens are propitious. Even if they were penniless, we *must* kill them if the omens order us to."

"Very well. I bow to your superior knowledge of the Law, and to your authority as the midwife of our rebirth."

Sandro, Colly and Jenny waited in cover, out of sight of each other, listening for the tinny local bus.

Colly had a brief word with Ishur Ghose, who had arrived by some unknown and separate means. He mentioned his friends.

"They are here to see fair play," he said. "To keep the ring, as we used to say."

"That's a great help," said Colly drily.

"Oh, you do not need help, Mr Tucker, I am *quite* sure. You and the Count have enjoyed a high-protein diet all your lives. The poor little specimens who will get off the bus have had *nothing* but carbohydrates."

Ishur Ghose hobbled away into the shadows.

Colly sauntered over to where Jenny sat invisible on her low mud wall. He reported the conversation. It was very odd and unsatisfactory.

The big man with silvering hair squatted in the darkness. A dozen men squatted in a close half-circle behind him. They were fifty yards from the village, hidden, at the edge of the jute-fields.

The big man held a brass jug, a few cowrie-shells, and a small pickaxe almost identical to the trenching-tool used by the British Army in the First War. Using these humdrum objects, he was completing a religious ceremony unknown to any orthodox sect of Hinduism.

At the end he softly intoned, in a language which was not any language of ordinary people in India: "Great Goddess, Universal Mother, if this our expedition be fitting in thy sight, vouchsafe us a sign of thine approbation."

The men behind repeated this prayer in the same strange tongue, quietly, sounding like sleepy bees.

They fell silent. They listened intently for the meaningful sound of crow or crane, of ass or jackal.

The open archway of a house at the edge of the village was brightly lit by an oil-lamp within. A figure came from the darkness into this patch of light. It was a young woman, heavily pregnant, with a waterpot on her head.

There was a collective gasp of joy, from the men squatting piously in the darkness, at this very best of all omens: this sign that the goddess approved and would assist the killing.

Then, in the distance, over the cry of insects and the babble and laughter just audible from the houses, and the shifting feet of cattle, they heard the rattle of the approaching bus.

Colly heard the bus. He stood up, stretched, and threw away his cigarette. He eased the gun in his shoulder-holster and fingered the cosh inside his sleeve. He stood by the trunk of a mango tree, seeming part of the trunk of the tree, waiting for the bus.

Sandro heard the bus. He uncoiled himself from the ground and brushed the khaki dust from his pants. He checked his weapons, and moved like a great cat into the angle of a ruined mud-built hut.

Jenny heard the bus. She was invisible, in dark jeans, dark shirt with sleeves to the wrists, and a dark scarf over her head. She was in reserve. Sandro and Colly would tackle the men, hold them up with guns, relieve them of their bundles. If there was trouble, Jenny would materialise behind the men with another gun. It was all right, it would work, if there were not too many men, and they had no guns, and they were not brave.

The big man with silvery hair had moved delicately to the edge of the village. His men were behind him.

He said softly, in the same strange language in which he had intoned his prayer, "Let the fight go as the fight goes, if there is any fight. Let such as are killed be killed, if it falls out thus. After, and only after, do we move."

There was a murmur of assent. The goddess was with them tonight, as she had told them by the omen of the woman great with child and carrying water.

* * *

Jenny saw the dim yellow headlights of the bus as it came out of a hollow onto the higher, flood-proof ground on which the village stood. Its engine thudded and protested at the slight gradient; its body rattled like a biscuit-tin on a roller-skate. It trundled to the sign at the edge of the village and stopped. The asthmatic engine cut.

Five men got off the bus. They were small men, stunted, undernourished, dirty. They carried all manner of bundles wrapped in blankets, cardboard boxes, and, between two, a tin trunk.

Jenny sighed with relief. This puny, pathetic enemy was an anticlimax. She welcomed the anticlimax.

The engine of the bus started again, the whirr of the starter turning at last into the gasp and thud of the engine. Its headlights brightened a little and it trundled away along the dirt road to the next village.

Before its single tail-light disappeared, Jenny saw two dark shapes advancing on the little group by the bus-stop. The beams of two big flashlights caught and impaled the five travellers. Colly's voice said something in careful Urdu. Utter dismay, almost comic, flooded into the little pinched dark faces of the five men. They dropped their bundles and raised their hands above their heads. Their wrists and arms were pitifully thin.

Jenny heard Colly say, "That seems to be our battle, chum. You cover them while I peek at the luggage."

"Okay," came Sandro's deep rumble.

There was silence, broken only by the rustle of oilskin and paper as Colly unwrapped a bundle.

Jenny heard another voice call softly from the darkness beyond. Their friends, their useless friends, waiting peacefully out of harm's way.

For the first time Jenny saw the friends: far more

than she expected—a dozen or more. Sandro had his back to them, gun in one hand and flashlight in the other. Colly was crouching in the dust, looking with his flashlight at the packets and bottles he had found.

The dozen men advanced delicately, saying nothing, their sandalled feet making no noise on the dust of the ground. One, bigger than the rest, a striking man with prematurely grey hair, came silently up behind Sandro. He stopped five feet away from him. He held a long pale scarf, just visible in the flashlight-glow reflected up from the ground. Three men were with him. Another three men silently approached Colly, keeping behind him. More men waited a few yards away.

There was no sign of Ishur Ghose.

Jenny had no idea what was happening, what these men were doing. But suddenly she had the sense that something was badly wrong: that something unthinkably terrible was about to happen.

Two

The big man with silvering hair held one end of his yellow-and-white scarf in each hand. He saw that his friend who stood behind the kneeling European had also his yellow-and-white scarf in both hands.

The big man opened his mouth to speak.

At that moment he was unspeakably astonished to see a woman, a girl, run out of the darkness into the glow of the flashlights: a girl carrying a gun, a girl with a pale-gold face and, escaping from a dark shawl, long bright-gold hair.

The girl cried in English, "Colly! Sandro! Behind you!"

The Italian turned like a dancer, the gun dwarfed by his enormous hand. The American was on his feet and his gun was in his hand.

The silver-haired man said, with smooth affability, in good English, "Please do not point those things at us. We might have intervened sooner, but we saw there was no need. Ishur Ghose said that there would be no need and he was perfectly correct. Are these the stolen drugs? My goodness, what a quantity. I expect you would appreciate a hand, carrying all this to your car. What are you going to do with your captives here?"

The atmosphere, charged for a few seconds with

an electric crackle of tension, relaxed into smiles and handshaking.

"Where is Ishur Ghose?" asked Colly.

"Oh, he went to sit down in one of the houses. He is not as young as he was and the drive out here was tiring for him."

"It was good of him to come at all. Good of you, too."

"He would not have missed it for anything. It has taken him back to his active days, you know. You gentlemen have done him quite a favour."

Presently Colly said, "I understand from Ishur Ghose that you and your friends are firm believers in non-violence."

"Like your Quakers. Yes, that is quite true."

"Do you mind my asking—what would you have done if ten guys with big cannons had got off that bus?"

The silver-haired man smiled. His smile had great warmth and charm. He said, "Of course it would have been a crisis of conscience. But we could not have stood by and watched two of you facing ten of them. Those odds would have been quite unsporting."

"Three of us," said Colly mildly.

The silver-haired man looked at Jenny. He was still smiling but there was something new in his smile. It was the smile of a child looking through a plate-glass window at the most desirable toy in the world.

"I am sorry," said Ishur Ghose. "I am truly sorry. I never dreamed that she would come. I have not been in contact with Europeans for so long that I had forgotten, I suppose, how different their women are from ours. I judge that she is an exceptional woman, even in Europe. Carrying a *gun*? That young unmarried girl? How very unseemly. But I am really sorry I made so grave a miscalculation."

"Do not be sorry," said the silver-haired man. "I am not sorry. I rejoice. The omen sent by the Goddess was not for us all but for me only. It must be so. Good fortune was promised, and the Goddess does not lie to her servants. Yet the expedition was a failure. What then meant the omen? What could it mean but that I have been shown my own future, my own felicity?"

"You are either interpreting the omen in order to justify your passion, or inducing passion in yourself in order to justify the omen," said Ishur Ghose severely. Then he smiled with great warmth and added, "Even if I do not quite accept that Kali sent the woman to you, I do accept that she will be the mother of cunning and valiant sons."

"Then I may proceed?"

Ishur Ghose laughed gently. "I can see that you will have no peace of spirit unless I permit you to proceed."

"They came prowling up like wolves," said Jenny. "So silent."

"So what, baby?" said Colly idly.

He was extremely pleased at the way things had gone. The middlemen were in police custody, but the American contact they tried to squeal about was already home in New York. Since he could be charged only on the information of known criminals, there was no question of extradition. There was no fuss at all. If John Tucker was upset at his stepson's precipitate departure he hid his grief pretty well. Not so his wife. Eleanor looked with bitter reproach at Colly and Jenny; she did not look at Sandro at all.

The fact that her son was a crook had not penetrated her consciousness.

"Indians don't prowl about silently," said Jenny. "Not groups of chums together. They jabber."

"Most do. But these are superior characters."

"Not judging by their clothes."

"They're followers of Gandhi. They were dressed better than he ever was. For God's sakes, darling, these people are friends of Ishur Ghose, and he's a party we know everything about. Decorated by the limey government, for what that's worth, friends in England, for what *that's* worth—"

"Yes, I know all that, but you didn't see them come out of the darkness at you."

"Not *at* us. They came *to* us."

"Four behind Sandro, three behind you."

"Well, they wanted to kind of spread the big hello between the two of us. Natural politeness, baby, that's all *that* means."

"*Will* you take this seriously?"

"No, baby, frankly I won't. We met a bunch of charming, peaceable, helpful, friendly guys, who would have joined in, in spite of their rules about not fighting, and who are vouched for by an old sweetheart who must be about the most reliable character-witness in India. My, what a long sentence. Subsidiary clauses and everything. My English teacher would be proud of me."

"Well, I'm not proud of you," said Jenny crossly. "I think you're being stupid as well as rude. I think you were just going to be killed."

"Horsefeathers, as a friend of mine used to say. If you weren't here I'd say something stronger. But if you weren't here I wouldn't *need* to say anything stronger."

Jenny was, at last, almost convinced that she had imagined the menace in the dark at the edge of the quiet mud-built village.

"But, Jemadar," said a man with a gentle, serious face, addressing, by his title, the leader of the group. "We do not understand the omen. We have all known all our lives, we drank with our mothers' milk, the meaning of the omens, and of all omens at such a moment we saw the best. Yet—"

"Yet?" asked the big handsome man with silvering hair.

"Yet a woman appeared from seeming nowhere, a woman who would have been witness of the slayings, a woman who would thus have had to be killed herself."

"You know as well as I, Sanghavi, that it was because our ancestors broke the ancient rules that they were almost destroyed by the British. And of all the broken laws that brought disaster on them, the most important related to women. When our ancestors started killing women, they brought upon themselves the just wrath of the Goddess, and it is only now that we have come to life again. And we are wiser. We have learned the terrible lessons of the past. We must and we shall keep the laws. We must not and shall not kill women."

"I know that, Jemadar. The woman could *not* be killed. Therefore, as matters lay, no one could be killed. Seven men were under our hand and they escaped us. Two we knew were rich, with golden objects in every pocket and money in leather folders. Five carried stolen goods worth lakh upon lakh of rupees. This was a disaster. Yet the Goddess has sent us the most encouraging of all her omens. *This* is what we do not understand."

"You did not see the woman, Sanghavi."

"Yes, I saw her, and my knees turned to water and my heart to stone at the ill fortune that she brought us."

"You did not see her with my eyes. In the short view—a night's *shikar,* some bodies to honour Kali, some money for her and for ourselves—the expedition was a failure. But in the long view the Goddess has shown me a prize beyond price. I am blessed among men. That is why the omen was good, Sanghavi."

"You mean . . . You cannot mean . . . The pale woman?"

"Yes."

"For a *wife?*"

"Of course. What else? We have all, always, lived virtuously. We have all, always, been remarkable among all the peoples of India for the tranquillity of our households, for the devotion of husband to wife and of child to parent. Is one of us to keep a woman as a prisoner in a house in the back streets of a city? Am I to take a concubine to the house in which my mother lives?"

"No. Such a thing would be unthinkable. But—"

"But?"

"It has been the custom of us all, always, to take a wife from our own people. A girl brought up in our mysteries, worshipping the Goddess as we worship her, speaking Ramasi."

"Yes. But there have been, in all ages, some wives from outside. When we have killed the father of a girl-child we have adopted the child and she has become the wife of one of us. And when one of us has met, on a *shikar,* a woman of shining beauty and high courage, a woman meet to breed sons for such as me . . . She came from the darkness, Sanghavi, unafraid, with a gun in her hand, seeing danger to her friends, seeing a dozen of us. She is a tiger with the beauty of an antelope. She has a head like the morning sun and eyes like the noonday sky."

"Your words sound strangely, Jemadar," said Sanghavi, troubled. "You, who are leader of us all under him who was the midwife of our rebirth . . . For you to conceive a passion of love for a woman of the *feringhi* . . . To be smitten thus, by as it were a madness, is strange at all times and for all men, but for *you,* and with *her* . . ."

"The Goddess set before our eyes a promise of great good fortune. And it was not, it was most evidently not, in the matter of the *shikar*."

"Oho. The Goddess herself sent that woman to that village?"

"What else meant the omen?"

"And the Goddess planted also in your heart the bright flower of love?"

"As it seems to me. What else meant the omen?"

"A woman like that," said Sanghavi, "will take some catching and some holding, Jemadar."

"Yes. But I have a way to catch her and a way to hold her."

John Tucker showed his gratitude by sending his guests to see all the sights. Sometimes Ishur Ghose joined these expeditions, a rich mine of curious information, a delightful if garrulous companion.

It was at his suggestion that they went to Kalighat, although he did not himself accompany them.

"A lot of this place," said Jenny, "seems beat-up but not old."

"Beat up?" repeated their guide, puzzled but trying hard. He was a neat-faced, smooth-spoken Bengali, with excellent but not perfect English, who worked

for the Calcutta office of one of the Tucker Group's
travel agencies.

"Dilapidated," explained Jenny, "but not what
you'd call antique."

"Oh yes! That is quite right. It is not an ancient
city of India, like Benares or Old Delhi. It was
founded by the East India Company, you know, by
the English. Before that it was only a ghat, you see, a
landing stage for the great temple."

"Which gave it the name, right?" said Colly.

"Oh yes! That is quite right."

"Ghat," said Jenny. "I don't get it. I haven't ghat
it. Ha bloody ha."

"Ha ha," said the guide politely. "It is Kali Ghat,
the landing place of Kali. It is where the goddess
came first to the earth. *Of course* she landed on
the bank of Gunga. Actually a small river called
Toly's Nala, but it is part of Gunga, like the Hooghly
here, and its waters are holy water, you know. Of
course there is a temple of Kali where she landed, at
Kalighat, her greatest temple. Very many pilgrims
come. Human sacrifices used to be pleasing to Kali,
but now goats only are sacrificed, very many goats,
a goat every few minutes. They chop off the heads of
the goats with one stroke."

"I'm not absolutely certain," said Jenny, "that's
something I absolutely have to see."

"You will not see anything like in Europe, Lady
Jennifer."

Jenny nodded dubiously. She admitted that there
was no point in coming to India and then not looking at it.

She looked at it, and smelled it, at the great temple at Kalighat. A large courtyard was packed with
beggars still more unnervingly revolting than those

of the streets of Calcutta, with holy saddhus, almost or entirely naked, their bodies coated with ashes and cowdung, and with pilgrims who seemed, by contrast, almost normal and civilized. The stench was appalling.

People of many kinds came here, it seemed, for many reasons. Jenny was surprised by the number of women at so grim a shrine, some very humble and simple, others not nearly so humble or, to all seeming, so simple.

"They are wives," explained the guide. "They pray for a child. They pray especially for a male child."

"To Kali?"

"Of *course* to Kali."

"But I thought she was Death."

"Of course, but she is life also. She is the *shakti* of Shiva. How can I explain that? She is the—female force, the energy, of her husband the god Shiva, who is the giver of life, you know, the reproducer. So wives will pray to her, *of course,* for conceiving babies."

"Of course," said Jenny weakly.

There were many subsidiary shrines. One housed a little red god who gave immunity from Mata, the smallpox, a god represented as a feeble but vicious donkey. In another shrine prayers were offered to a five-headed cobra who armoured the faithful against snakebite.

Among the swarms of the very poor there were a few well-dressed men, glossy and sleek, come to pray for success in their business transactions. There were students, including budding scientists and doctors, come to beg Kali's help in their examinations. But they were a handful amid the thousands of beggars, holy men and pilgrims. Nearly all the pilgrims were gaunt men with hot, sick eyes; they were crying in

Bengali and Hindi and Punjabi and Tamil and fifty lesser languages; they were waiting with twitching impatience for the next sacrifice to Kali.

Kali herself was black. Her hands and eyes were red, her hair matted, her breasts blood-daubed, her teeth long and evil, like fangs. Priests waited with knives. A man hurried up, just managing to keep hold of a terrified kid which bleated and struggled and almost escaped. It did not escape. As its blood larded the base of the horrible idol a moan of worship came from all sides, from the stinking crowd of pilgrims.

Of whom, it seemed to Jenny, there were two distinct sorts.

Most were very humble people, underfed, stunted, of low caste, dark-skinned, on whom the emotional effect of the sacrifice was visibly overwhelming. They twitched, shrieked, frothed at the mouth; the eyes of some swivelled until only the whites were visible; some fell in fits onto the dirty ground. They showed uninhibited hysteria, a shameless surrender to group emotion. They were like young girls screaming and fainting at a pop-idol, or the most primitive Africans in self-induced trances after their drumming and dancing.

But there were others, a few others. Not the sleek businessmen, nor the intense, abstracted students, but other pilgrims. In dress they were identical to the pathetic, fanatical majority, but they were better physical specimens, taller and stronger, better fed. They were of the languages and castes of all the rest, but they were different from all the rest: they were just a little different in manner.

They watched the sacrifice, not with shrieks and thrashings of the limbs, but in sober and reverent approval.

Another goat, wildly bleating, was brought to the feet of Kali. Jenny looked away. She looked again at the pilgrims.

She felt rather than saw the almost invisible contrast between the simple, near-bestial fanatics and the sober worshippers. The first were horrible and frightening, as mad animals are horrible and frightening, but they did not seem dangerous because they were not mysterious. Everything about them was obvious. There were no secrets. Nothing was held back. They freely and shrilly declared their faith, their devotion, their excitement, their purpose in being in this place of blood and terror.

But the others, the gravely reverent minority? There were faces of sharp intelligence among them: of observation, decision, action. They worshipped, but their eyes were not glazed. They prayed, but their lips were not foam-flecked. They intoned, but they did not scream.

They were mysterious. Much about them was unobvious. There were secrets, there must be, behind those calm and clever faces.

Colly said to their guide: "I understand that a good many Hindus—uh—tend to deprecate what we just saw. Forgive me if that's an impertinent question."

"No, Mr Tucker. You are quite right *of course*. Kali can be worshipped in a decent way *of course*, shall I say an adult and civilized way, and not like that. The poor little young goats, such a noise, and those very bad men screaming like green parrots."

"Are they very bad men, the Kali-worshippers?"

"Oh yes, those ones, you can see with your own eyes, they are the very dregs, you know. No person of intelligence or education takes part in a pujah like

that. Of course it is interesting from an anthropolog-
ical viewpoint, which is why your friend suggested
that I should kindly bring you to see it. It is the
very dregs, you know. I personally believe that most
of these chaps are half mad. A person of any sophistication would see at once that it is all the most
awful rot, you know."

Jenny agreed that it was the most awful rot. Colly
and Sandro remained fascinated by the primitive
paganism of the world's oldest great religion, but
Jenny had had enough. She went out into the forecourt of the temple and sat down in the shade of a
wall.

The crowd pressed round her, closer and closer. It
was as though the forecourt had been filled by an
immense new influx of pilgrims, forcing those already
there into the walls and corners. Jenny could not see
if this had happened. There was a great deal of
noise, of incessant high-voiced crying in a variety of
languages. The crowd pressed round Jenny so that
she had to stand up: there was no longer room to sit.

Some parts of the mob she had seen in the temple
would have frightened her, pressing round her like
this: the wild-eyed ones, the dung-daubed fanatics.
But she was not yet frightened because the crowd
round her were quiet and well-conducted people. One
or two smiled at her, diffidently, as though apologizing
for causing her inconvenience and discomfort.

But they squeezed round her very tightly.

She began to feel an onrush of claustrophobia. She
fought it down. Panic in such a place would be very
ill-judged.

"Steady," she said to herself, half aloud.

Hardly was the word out, and as though the word
was a trigger, when her face was suddenly smothered

in a damp cloth with a strong, sweet smell. At the same time her arms were held to her sides and other hands grabbed her ankles.

Four of them, she thought, as she struggled to free her legs and arms, and fought the overpowering anaesthetic on the cloth. The hands that held her were as firm as rocks: yet it occurred to her, on the edge of swoon, idiotically, that there was something considerate about the hands: they were not hurting her: they were careful not to hurt her.

She seemed to swing through great arcs across a black sky, and then to plummet into a black sea.

Three

"No dice," said Colly heavily.

Sandro nodded.

They had looked round casually at first, then searched with mounting irritation that turned into fright and then to despair.

Jenny would not have gone away without telling them; never; not of her own free will.

They in English and halting Urdu, their guide in Bengali, had asked hundreds of pilgrims and worshippers and sightseers if they had seen a young European woman with yellow hair. A few remembered seeing her. None had seen her leave.

The police were on their way.

The police were formidable and thorough. They disciplined the volatile mob of pilgrims with the threat and occasional use of long bamboo staves, ironbound. They covered all the same ground and asked all the same questions and came out with the same answer: nothing.

A description of the missing girl was circulated and the British Embassy was informed.

Jenny was conscious at first only of movement. For a long time she was aware, in her lucid moments, of travelling. She did not know in what direction, or by what mode of transport. She could see nothing. Something—a scarf or soft bandage—was tied tightly over her eyes. It was not uncomfortable. She could move her limbs, but only languidly. They felt intolerably heavy: movement was not worth the immense effort.

There were soft voices about her, the voices of several men, speaking an unfamiliar language.

Sandro and Colly went later in the day to Police Headquarters.

"I wonder," said a senior official, "if this shocking affair could relate in any way to our principal headache at the moment."

"Kidnapping?"

"Perhaps. But we think not. People have disappeared as though kidnapped, but—"

"Who have disappeared?" asked Colly.

"Hundreds of people."

"Hundreds?"

"This is in the strictest confidence. I would not be telling you about it had I not been instructed to do so by the Ministry itself. Yes, I am afraid so. Hundreds. People of all kinds. That is to say, men of all kinds. In the last six months, in all parts of India. A group of men unknown to each other has, let us say, got aboard a train at the Howrah Station here in Calcutta to go to Patna or Benares or Delhi, and simply disappeared. Or, to put it more precisely, simply not arrived."

"And this is a new thing?" asked Colly.

"Not *entirely* new. In any country people disappear. They run away from home because they are tired of their wives, and start a new life in a distant place. Or they fall into a river and get stuck under a stone. But what I am now referring to is on a scale which is new. Oh yes, new and gravely disturbing."

"There's a town in the United States," said Colly slowly, "with a higher official rainfall than anyplace else, not because more rain falls, but because the City Fathers look at the rain gauge twenty times a day."

The police official looked at him blankly.

"I'm sorry," said Colly. "I guess I'm in shock and I didn't explain myself too well. It's like disease, though. There's more typhoid reported in some places not because there *is* more but because the Chamber of Commerce lets the doctors admit it. So it goes on record, like that rainfall. There's more of other diseases recorded in other places simply because the doctors diagnose them. Maybe people in this country are getting better at noticing when their folks go missing. Maybe they're more ready to report it because they're not so frightened of you guys."

The official's face cleared. "I understand. Your point was obscure to me at first, but it is well taken, Mr Tucker. It is quite true that the incidence of a particular crime, statistically speaking, like that of a particular disease, can be a picture of the distribution of alert police officers, or doctors, rather than that of specialist criminals or the relevant virus. It may even be, in a strange sense, the fashion to diagnose a particular disease, though not, perhaps, a crime. The same thought *of course* occurred to me when these disappearances began to be reported in numbers. It also, I happen to know, occurred to colleagues as far away as Bombay and Amritsar and Mysore. But we are now certain it is not so. We cannot prove that there were not 500 unreported disappearances last year, but we can see no reason why families all over India should suddenly take to reporting disappearances which, for reasons equally inexplicable, they were previously reluctant to report."

Colly nodded. The official's mastery of English was

rather irritatingly self-conscious, but what he said was convincing.

He went on, "I mentioned a group of men who climbed onto a train here and never arrived in Benares. I was citing an actual case, perfectly typical of this disturbing phenomenon. Five men with nothing whatever in common, none of whom knew any of the others, ascended into the same part of a train. There was also seen in the same carriage a group of pilgrims. The latter may have arrived. At least, if they did not, their non-arrival was not reported to us. The five men we do know about disappeared without trace. One was a clerk in a big store in the Chowringhee, visiting an aged relative who went to Benares to die but had not at that period yet died. The second was a minor official of the Department of Health on an official mission connected with the control of malaria. The third was a functionary of the railway itself. The fourth was a merchant who sold brass vessels in Benares, returning from a visit to Calcutta on a perfectly legitimate errand of which we have details. The fifth and last was an official in the Benares city government also visiting Calcutta, for a reason that was not so perfectly legitimate, I regret to say. All these five were seen onto the train by friends or family at the Howrah Station, and they were all to be met at the other end. But they were not met, because they were not on the train."

"They got off the train on the way," said Sandro.

"Possibly. But all five together? And why?"

"There were pilgrims in the same car," said Colly, "but you don't know whether they got there or not?"

"Thousands of pilgrims doubtless arrived at that time. Benares is the holy city of India, Mr Tucker. There are hundreds of thousands of pilgrims there constantly, and more arrive with every train and with every bus and bullock-cart."

"Were any of the five you know about carrying a lot of money?"

"We opine that none would be carrying a great quantity of specie. All must have been carrying some."

"Enough to be worth stealing?"

"One anna is worth stealing if you are very hungry, Mr Tucker."

"Might any of the five have done a deliberate bunk? The man in the store, having dipped his fingers in the till? The municipal official?"

"We think not. Certainly not all five. That would be a coincidence to stretch one's credulity, don't you agree?"

"Maybe it is not coincidence," said Sandro. "Maybe they did know each other, secretly, and planned something together."

"An obvious possibility, Count. It is the first thing we tried to establish. But if there is the smallest link between any two of the five it remains totally hidden. We have a copious dossier on each of the five men. We interviewed a large number of people in connection with each man. All the time we were endeavouring to establish any link between them, and any reason why any one of them might have wished to disappear. We found nothing."

"The Benares city official?" asked Colly. "Suppose someone was wise to him?"

"He was the *last* one to run away. He was on to what they call a good thing. On a modest scale, but even so deplorably normal in this country. It was a small regular transaction connected with the city tax paid by merchants with stalls in the market. Who did *not* include, incidentally, the vendor of brass pots. The local police only uncovered the small pecula-

tion after the man disappeared, and because he disappeared."

"These people could have been kidnapped."

"In theory, yes. But they were not rich men. A
large ransom could not have been demanded. And in
the event no ransom has been demanded in the four
months since this particular episode."

"Then you think they're dead."

"We do not know what else to think."

"You think these mysterious pilgrims did it?"

"If they were in truth pilgrims, no."

"Why?"

"Pilgrims do not kill people. If you go to Benares
to wash away your sins, Mr Tucker, you do not on
the way add murder to those sins."

"That's logical. But if they were false pilgrims?"

"That is the theory to which we keep returning.
But it is an answer which answers nothing, not who,
not how, not why."

"You say there have been lots of cases like this?"

"Nearly a thousand people have disappeared."

"*What?*"

"Nine hundred and thirty-two, and all in the last
six months."

Jenny's senses and brain became over the hours a
little, a very little, more receptive. She became aware
of more things.

She became aware of her clothes. She did not know
what she was wearing but she knew it was unfamiliar. It smelled and felt strange. She was wrapped in
something large and loose and enveloping; it covered
her head and most of her face as well as all her body.
It was hot but perfectly comfortable. Although something covered her face, it was so arranged that she
could breathe without difficulty.

She became aware that she was treated, by the invisible strange-talking men, with gentleness and respect. This was not at first obvious but after a time it became unmistakable; after a time, and after her emergence into longer periods of consciousness, and periods of heightened consciousness. It was as though she were a patient, the victim of crippling accident or grave illness, being looked after by concerned and expert doctors; or as though she were a great lady being cosseted by chamberlains. It was pleasant.

She became aware of the atmosphere which surrounded her. It was an atmosphere of goodwill. There was nothing in it inimical, no trace of threat. She felt affectionate concern, a firm kindliness. Whoever these people were, they were friends, they wished her well, they were looking after her, they would let no harm come to her.

It was utterly puzzling, but Jenny's brain was, like her limbs, sluggish with weariness or illness. She felt very stupid. The effort to think was too great. For the time being she could only lie, gently jolted and vibrated by the fact of travelling, being ministered to by kind men with gentle hands and murmuring, incomprehensible voices.

"All these people," said Colly, "disappeared during journeys?"

"Stretching the word somewhat, yes. If we take a journey to include going for a short walk. These people all set off at one end and failed to arrive at the other end."

"Travelling how? All possible ways?"

"Not by air. But in all other ways. By train, bus, car, taxi, bicycle, cart, and on foot. Also in boats. Not in big ships, you understand, but in small boats."

"No pattern then?"

"None that we can see, except negatively. The people who go by air still arrive at their destinations."

"And the people who disappeared were all groups of strangers?"

"Not at all. A great number disappeared all alone. That is to say, no other person was reported missing at the same time and place. And a great number were in groups, such as colleagues, or three brothers together, or a father and son."

"No pattern."

"None, Mr Tucker."

"Brothers. Father and son. Never sisters, mothers, daughters, wives?"

"No. The persons reported missing have been without exception male."

Colly and Sandro looked at each other.

"That's odd," said Colly, turning back to the official. "I've seen a lot of women wearing heavy silver jewellery. Gold, too. Necklaces, anklets, earrings, nose-jewels. And I guess some carry money, don't they?"

"Indeed they do, if they go to a market to buy food, or travel by train."

"Those five on the train to Benares were all different. I mean, different jobs, different social levels. Are all the rest different too? Haphazard like that? People who just happened to be there when whatever it is struck?"

"Obviously we have tried to find a pattern there —anything—geographic, socio-economic, trade or profession, caste, religion, age, language, height, colouring, dress, political affiliation, sexual proclivities. But we did not find one. There is no pattern. The people who disappear are, with one qualification, a fair cross-section of Indian males."

"What's the qualification?"

"A logical one. More people have disappeared of

the kind more likely to travel. I refer to businessmen, government officials, employees of the railway or of the bus companies, and persons who can afford to go away on holiday. More of such persons have been reported missing than farmers or local storekeepers who are not likely to travel. On the whole slightly richer persons have been disappearing at a higher rate than the very poor."

"They travel more."

"Yes, of course. It may also be a factor that they are visibly more worth robbing. At the same time, a certain number of very, very poor men have disappeared just as completely as moneylenders from Bombay."

"Foreigners?"

"Very few, I am thankful to say. No white persons at all."

"Until now."

"Yes. Three Americans have disappeared."

"Ah?"

"All black. Two near a place called Aurangabad, which I do not myself know at all. They hired bicycles, in order to inspect some temples in a hillside. People saw them leave. They were not seen at the temples and they did not return. One was an architect, one a medical student. Both came from Los Angeles. Both were on vacation. Both are said to have had watches, cameras, and a little money. It is utterly deplorable that friendly visitors from America should suffer . . ."

"They were killed?"

"We must assume so. We can think of no other explanation. But if you knock a man off his bicycle, kill him, and take his watch and camera, why go to such extraordinary lengths to conceal the body."

"The crime's not discovered so soon."

"It is not identified as the crime of murder so soon. But serious trouble is reported very soon. If a foreign visitor says, 'I will be back for the evening meal,' and he does not come back, some person will inevitably blow the proverbial whistle."

"I see what you mean. And you're bound to suspect a mugging anyway . . . What about the other black American?"

"He was with a group of Indians, six men in all. They were a party of agricultural chemists visiting a village in Rajasthan, a semi-desert area where the authorities are trying to raise the yield of the crops. The six went off with three of the villagers, making nine men in all, to inspect the fields near the village. They walked a short way out of the village, in the evening, and none of them came back. They walked off the edge of the world."

"Silly to ask if there was any trace, any clue."

"If we are to believe the local police, there was none."

"No people were seen around?"

"Of course there were people about, Mr Tucker. They were near a large village. Strangers came by, and quite evidently killed them. We have not succeeded in establishing a motive."

"Why strangers? Why not other people from the village?"

"It was evening. Everybody had finished their work and was getting ready for the evening meal. Every soul in the village had an alibi ten times over. The killers, if the men were killed, must have been strangers. There were strangers. Strangers were seen."

"Ah."

"But nobody looked at them. Nobody knew that there was any reason to look at them until the party failed to return from their walk. Finally the people of the village became alarmed and tried to search. But by this time of course it was dark. In the morning they found nothing. A most meticulous police search revealed no trace of any struggle, no unusual marks on the ground, no bodies of course. The missing persons might have been vapourised."

"Has any property turned up belonging to any of the missing people?"

"That is a good question. Yes, it has. But not much, and not in any way to incriminate anybody. Presumably a good deal of stolen property is in circulation. I refer to cameras and transistor radios and watches, perhaps expensive shoes and silk shirts, but very little has been traced back."

"That's unusual. Crooks are generally careless about that."

"Yes. It is one of the more disquieting aspects. The absence of such carelessness argues discipline and organization. It suggests criminal sophistication in the people responsible for all this."

"Yes, it does," said Colly. "But why are people like that bothering with poor villagers on the edge of the desert? Why aren't they robbing rich American tourists?"

"We do not know why. And I must admit that we do not know why 900 people have disappeared, presumed murdered, without one single body being found."

"I suppose bodies *are* found?"

"Of course, but they are not missing. They are not on this list but on a different list. There may be a mystery but it is a different kind of mystery. Of course there are murders in India. We have a population of 500 million people, and some of them are bound to kill each other in the way of trade, or jealousy, or religious zeal. The body in such cases is practically always found, and usually straight away. But the ordinary murder of one man by another, for whatever reason, is a far cry from nine men disappearing without trace a short distance outside a Rajasthani village."

"And this is still going on?"

It was still going on. A telephone message came, with news of another disappearance. Far away in the Punjab, almost in Pakistan, a small local bus had been driven into Dharmkot in the late evening. Eight particular passengers were expected to be on the bus. Other passengers were on the bus, but not these eight. The driver was not the usual driver. He was unknown to anybody. He faded away after he stopped the bus and was not seen again. There were descriptions of him, but not good ones. The passengers on the bus also faded away. No one knew any of them. No one in Dharmkot admitted to having been on the bus. The eight passengers were known to have entered the bus at various villages outside Dharmkot; it was known that they intended to ride into the town; they had not done so. They had disappeared. The proper driver of the bus had also disappeared. None of the nine missing men was rich, though none was indigent. They were marginally worth robbing. Obviously the man who had driven the bus into Dharmkot, and his passengers, had caused the disappearance of the others. Presumably they had murdered them. Motive, method, and the disposition of the bodies were all equally obscure. As to the identity of the presumed murderers, there were no leads of any kind, except a few inadequate and contradictory descriptions. The whole thing was totally puzzling to the local and provincial police and to the ministry in Delhi. It was totally puzzling, but it was

exactly in line with all the other disappearances of
the previous six months.

And, apart from the matter of her sex and race,
Jenny's disappearance was totally in line with them
too.

The Railway Police at Ghazipur had copies of a
description of a young lady from foreign-side who
had run away or been raped or killed. They inspected
carefully all the people who got off the train from
Patna and the Calcutta line.

From a special reserved compartment came four
men of whom two were doctors and two medical orderlies. The orderlies wore neat, well-pressed white
cotton clothes. They carried a stretcher, on which a
small figure lay under wrappings. The senior doctor
was a tall man with a mane of silvering hair and a
look of solemn distinction. He fussed about the
stretcher, enjoining care on the orderlies. He told
the police that his patient was a lady of extreme age,
a Maharani when India still had such anachronistic
extravagances. She had insisted on pilgrimage to
Benares, which was after all only fifty miles away.
He had reluctantly consented, on condition that she
was with him and under his care. Even so her religious observances had utterly exhausted her. He
would give her intravenous glucose. She clung to life
with great tenacity, wishing to see the eldest of her
great-grandchildren married. She was a great lady
and had once, it was said, been fatally beautiful. All
the papers were available in the doctor's case, if the
gentlemen of the Railway Police wished to inspect
them. They must not, however, disturb the patient,
who was under mild sedation. The doctor was very
loquacious. He wasted the time of the Railway Police, who were glad to see the last of him.

The party was met by a private ambulance with a uniformed Sikh driver.

Colly wrote to Jenny's mother. He had known the Countess of Teffont for many years and was very fond of her. His recent visit to the enormous house in Wiltshire was the latest of many. He had often been there, to ride the family's horses, catch the trout in its rivers, and give a misleading impression to its neighbours of frivolous sloth.

Colly wrote saying that Jenny had gone off somewhere, possibly with someone, but that he and Sandro would shortly find her.

He did not believe what he wrote. He did not think Jenny's mother would believe it either.

Four

Jenny was dimly aware of being carried through crowds, of being slid into the back of a vehicle. Her friends were still around her. They spoke to each other words which were not Urdu, Bengali, Hindi or any other language Jenny had ever heard.

The vehicle started. Jenny felt frequent tight turns, and heard continuous babbling, hooting, ringing of bells. They were in the narrow, winding streets of a town.

The men were making curious movements, throwing out an arm or leg, as it seemed to Jenny, as though puppets tugged by strings. Over the other noises of the vehicle and the streets, Jenny could hear the rustle of fabrics, the squeak of shoe-sole and the metal floor, the zip of a bag. It occurred to her, in a flash of lucidity, that they were changing their clothes.

"We have to assume it's part of the same thing," said Colly.

"But," said Ishur Ghose, "if I remember correctly, you told me that this—organization, if it is one—has never, ah, taken a woman."

"They have maybe changed their rules," said Sandro.

"Or it's a different bunch," said Colly. "Can we believe that?"

Ishur Ghose shrugged. "Lady Jennifer is a beautiful young lady. To an Indian her fairness makes her still more beautiful. There are millions of Indians who are very frustrated, very inhibited. It is an unfortunate effect of Hinduism. My years of contact with the British made me in some measure a free-thinker, like Mr Nehru, and I can be objective about it. Men are simply not allowed intimate relations with a woman, except young married men. Except in the early years of marriage, Indian men are supposed to be celibate. It is not a natural state of life, is it? So they become very hot and lustful. You know that, after petty theft, the most frequent of all crimes in India is rape? Also there are millions of Indians who are very poor, and she looks, you know, *not* poor. I am not suggesting anything. I do not think you can leap to the assumption that it is part of what the police were telling you about."

"Jenny's disappearance," said Colly slowly, "is one of 900 disappearances in the last six months."

"What? What is this? What are you saying?"

"You don't know about it?" asked Colly, very surprised.

"Not about 900 people. Not about a thing on *that* scale. Tell me."

Sandro told him.

Ishur Ghose said, "I had not heard the extent of this. I am very out of touch. Almost a hermit now, busy with old books and memories almost equally old. I hardly ever read a newspaper, and I never listen to the radio. This contraption"—he waved a brown claw at his hearing-aid—"is not well adapted, for some reason, to the sounds made by the radio. It is no deprivation to me. I would rather read about Shah Jehan and Aurangzebe and Sivaji than about the leaders of the Congress Party who have grown so very rich by not following the precepts of their founder."

"Even so," said Colly, "I would have thought you'd hear things on the grapevine. I mean, your old mates in the service."

"Good gracious no. I was quite discredited. Remember who I was working for. People like me were not at all popular with the new rulers of India. I suppose, in any case, the minimum of publicity has been given to this phenomenon you have described. Did you say over 900 disappearances in six months? Panic could be caused by a thing like that, and this country is difficult enough to keep calm at the best of times. They are somewhat volatile, my fellow countrymen, and deeply superstitious. There might be a witch-hunt started, you know, with the sort of consequences which followed partition. Wholesale slaughter of minority groups. It is always possible in India. Remember Bangla Desh. Suppose the Sikhs were blamed for these disappearances, or the Parsees, or the communists. There could be a blood bath, totally unjustified and illogical, but just as disagreeable for the victims. Oh yes, the less said in public the better about such a thing."

"Makes it harder to get any answers," said Colly heavily. "Makes it harder to go looking for anybody."

"I am afraid that is quite true."

The vehicle stopped. Jenny heard the door open, and felt herself lifted. She felt bright sun for a moment, hot on the wrappings which covered her; then warm, crowded darkness. She felt herself being hoisted up steep stairs. There were many soft voices, the high chirruping voices of young women. There was a smell of bhang, tobacco, incense and cheap scent.

After a long pause, heavy with misery and foreboding, Colly said, "Nobody who disappeared turned up. Not yet. Not in the whole history of this thing. Not one in over 900. No one turned up dead or alive. They stayed disappeared."

"*Si*," said Sandro.

"India goes from Karakoram to Cormorin, 2000 miles. From Calcutta to Kutch, 1300 miles. There's mountain, desert, jungle, places so remote you can only get to them a few weeks in the year. More than 400 million population. Some people so isolated only one hundred in all speak the language. Some in enormous overcrowded cities like anthills. Some who keep their women veiled and behind locked doors. Even if Jenny's alive—"

"We must believe she is alive."

"We must try. Even if she is, the only way we'll find her is if they get in touch with us, wanting a deal, a ransom."

"I think," said Ishur Ghose hesitantly, "I am right in saying they have not done that before."

"No. Not once. Even though they took a few rich men whose families would have paid a big ransom. Kidnapping has got to be a big industry in a few places like Italy, but these guys are not in that racket. Or haven't been, up until now."

"If they are still not in that racket—"

"Then," said Colley, "they won't get in touch with us."

"What will you do?" asked Ishur Ghose.

"I don't know. Go look, but I don't know where."

* * *

The Moon of Delight was bored. She lolled among the cushions of her dark little room, smoking an American cigarette given her by her last client and playing with her bracelets. She was the most beautiful of the girls in the House of Whistling Birds (so called because its stairs and passages were always full of birdlike whispers and giggles) and for a full day and night she had done no business. The richest of her regular lovers was ill with a pernicious vomit: a business rival had, doubtless, achieved by sorcery what he had failed to achieve in the way of trade.

She heard footsteps on the dirty stairs, the footfalls of several men. Was this business at last? Or were these more of the stupid oxen who preferred the painted lips and sullen eyes of some of the younger girls? She looked through the arch, its curtain hooked back, out into the dim-lit passage, and saw the tall man his friends called Feringhia. She was disappointed. Neither he nor any of those that came here with him were customers, at least in the ordinary sense. They were courteous people, soft-spoken, not ungenerous, but they were clients neither of her own nor of any of the other girls in the house.

Feringhia saluted the Moon, inclining his head with its mane of silvery hair. She gestured languidly back, as she had long ago been taught, her bracelets jangling. Feringhia was dressed as a poor farmer, although the Moon knew he was not poor and guessed he was not a farmer. He glanced back over his shoulder, gesturing to someone behind him.

He said to the Moon, "Sheelah will want you."

The Moon nodded. It was business, though not the usual kind of business of the House of Whistling Birds.

Feringhia disappeared along the passage. He was followed by two men, also seeming farmers, in dhotis

and big red turbans. They carried between them a
litter with a person or body on it. The person was
invisible under white sheets. A fourth man, known
by sight to the Moon, followed the litter-bearers.

The Moon got up from the cushions. She stubbed
out her cigarette on the floor. She followed the men
down the narrow passage to Sheelah's room and
pushed through the door-curtain.

The room was in half darkness. The window on to
the balcony was shuttered. The cushions were as usual
strewn untidily over the floor, with among them a
few hookahs. The room smelled of stale tobacco and
bhang. The litter was on the floor, its burden still
covered with sheets.

Sheelah, lying propped on cushions and smoking
her favourite small hookah, looked fatter and crazier
than ever. She was immense. She had once, it was
said, been as slim and beautiful as the Moon herself,
a breaker of hearts, a driver to madness, an earner
of great sums in gold and heavy baskets of jewels.
Now she was old and grossly fat, vast-armed, many-
chinned, dewlapped like Shiva's own bulls. She was
also blind, owing to the effects of disease or accident
or witchcraft; her eyes were not like eyes, but like
peeled eggs. She still made good money, not as a har-
lot but as a witch. She was known to few, but those
few paid well. The Moon was her apprentice, her
assistant and pupil, her chela, because the Moon's own
beauty would fade, and she would no longer be desirable to the smooth officials and businessmen.

Sheelah was dressed neither in a sari, like the
Moon, nor in a tight immodest European dress like
some of the girls, but was wrapped in scores of yards
of what looked like dirty butter-muslin. She was a
mass of gold ornament: her thick wrists and hamlike
arms were jammed with heavy bangles; both drop-

sical ankles carried half a dozen circlets; there was gold hanging massively from her ear-lobes, transfixing her nostril, circling her neck, pendant on her brow. Her bangles crashed together like cars colliding in a narrow street.

She looked sightlessly towards Feringhia. She said, in the little girlish voice that came so strangely from her vast bulk, "The message spoke of colour that will last half a year."

"Yes."

"It is ready."

She turned her face towards the Moon, although she could not have heard the girl enter, nor known in what quarter of the room she stood. She said, "The brazen bowl with turquoises at the rim. The green cloth."

The Moon slipped into the little room, hardly larger than a wardrobe, in which Sheelah kept the supplies and implements of her trade. The bowl with turquoises set in the rim was ready on a shelf. It was full of a viscous, blueish liquid. The green cloth beside it was no rag, but a length of the finest Benares silk. The Moon would dearly have liked it—such stuff was rare now that the Mohammedan weavers had nearly all left Varanasi—and it was a shame that it should be indelibly dyed. But she would not have dreamed of disobeying Sheelah, who could tell colour through her fingertips. She took the silk, with the bowl, back to Sheelah in the main room. She set them down beside Sheelah, who, without groping, touched each to be sure of its position.

Sheelah nodded again to the Moon, who struck a match and lit powdered incense in a flat dish. Smoke belched from the dish; the burning incense crackled like hot fat in a pan.

Sheelah gestured to the men to leave the room.

They did so at once, in obedient silence. The last
to go out into the passage carefully drew shut the
heavy door-curtain. The Moon knew that the men
would be stationed outside the curtain until Sheelah
had finished, and that they would on no account whatever allow anyone into the room, or peep into the
room themselves. They were serious men, who respected the decencies; they were sensible men, hard
headed, who would not pay an expensive witch and
then jeopardise her spells by prying.

At another signal from Sheelah—a gesture which
set her bracelets clashing together like cooking-pots
hanging from a donkey—the Moon lifted the sheets
from the figure on the litter.

The Moon gasped. She had not expected a woman
—still less a girl no older than herself—still less a
very beautiful European with hair of a gold brighter
than any of Sheelah's.

The Moon stripped all the clothes off the girl, leaving only the bandage on her eyes; she looked down
at last, with bitter envy, at the pearl-white, pearl-
smooth body. The white fingers twitched; one white
arm moved slowly, feebly, without purpose. The girl
was drugged, but not enough.

As though Sheelah had heard or felt the small
movement, she hoisted herself awkwardly into a
crouch beside the litter. She put her fingers on the
brow of the girl and very gently stroked it, her fingertips describing small circles. She murmured, in
her high, girlish voice, a mesmeric command that the
white one should sleep.

The twitching fingers were still. The slim white
arms and long, beautiful legs were as flaccid as those
of a drowned corpse. The breathing was regular,
deep, very slow. Sheelah took the bandage off the girl's
eyes, which were fast shut.

The room was full of the aromatic, dizzying smoke from the incense-dish. There was no sound except the sizzle of the incense burning.

With the Moon's help, Sheelah anointed every part, every square millimetre of the white girl's body with the dye from the dish set with turquoises. She did not wipe, but dabbed with the green silk cloth. The Moon took the cloth and dabbed between the girl's toes, and into the convolutions of her ears, because Sheelah's fingers were too thick for the narrow places.

The hair was dyed, almost strand by strand, with a thinner fluid from a different vessel.

All the time she worked, Sheelah's little high voice intoned invocations to demons and, though she was a kind of Hindu, to the djinns of Islam. The Moon made the responses in a voice which she lowered to a murmur from its usual shrillness. The invocations protected the girl from all kinds of danger, from discovery, from the premature fading of the dye, from death in childbed, from typhoid and smallpox, from the police. The invocations were also hypnotic; their purpose was to remove from the mind of the white girl, who was no longer white, all memories and personality, and leave it like a sheet of blank paper.

Sheelah had never read books by Western psychologists: she did not know that what she was doing was impossible—that experience reaches so far down into the personality, changing or deeply engraving all that it touches, that to try to eradicate it all, induce total amnesia, is ridiculous.

But by the same token, no Western psychologists had heard of Sheelah, and few knew anything about the ancient hypnotism which she practised. Had they done so, some books would not have been written, and many would have been written differently. It

was not the first time, not by a score, that Sheelah
had drawn out with her fingers and voice all the
writing inscribed by experience within a skull, leaving blankness to be written on anew. She had not
failed before. Not by so much as the twitch of an
eyelid had any of the score shown that they retained
any of that which she had removed: not by the gen-
tlest thumping of the heart when faced with the
face of wife or mother: not by the smallest catching
of the breath when confronted by dead child or live
enemy.

Sheelah had never failed: but Sheelah had never
used her skills on a European, on a sophisticated,
highly-educated, tough-minded Anglo-Saxon woman,
brought up to independence of spirit, and with years
behind her of quick decision, violent action, and an
inbuilt refusal to be defeated or subjugated.

Colly and Sandro sat down to a late dinner, but
neither could eat. They needed food, because they
needed all their strength, but they could force nothing down.

Colly, looking across the table at Sandro, saw in
the familiar face a weariness which was unusual to
it: a despair which was quite new to it. It was possible to hope, but only just. It was impossible to
plan. It would be impossible to search even one small
Indian town, even with full and massive police co-
operation, let alone the whole subcontinent.

And police co-operation was a dubious asset. A
big police search meant warrants, documentation,
clerks and files, messages; therefore a leak; therefore
forewarning. Ishur Ghose had made this point and it
was a good one. The bigger the police operation, the
more certain that Jenny, if she was still alive, would
be spirited away and hidden somewhere else.

Losing Jenny was unthinkable. The thought of life without her was unendurable. Life with her was difficult for Colly, an unceasing heartache, because he loved her, and had loved her for years, and would love her until he died. She loved him too, as devotedly and enduringly, but it was a different sort of love. There was a fatal difference. Sometimes knowledge of this was better than nothing, and sometimes much worse. There was nothing either of them could do about it.

Sandro was in exactly the same situation. He had been in love with Jenny a little longer than Colly, because he had known her a little longer. They never discussed it. It was perhaps the only subject they never discussed. But each knew exactly how the other felt.

Each knew that the other now felt a sense of loss like amputation, worse than any amputation, worse than any death.

Well, it was possible to hope. But only just. And hope was the only thing it was possible to do.

At last the colouring was finished, back and front, body and hair, the little folds below the eyelids, the tiny wrinkles over the knuckles.

Between them, Sheelah and the Moon propped the girl into a sitting position among the cushions, her back to the wall of the room. The Moon oiled and combed the long, shiny-black hair, then twisted it into a single thick plait. She covered the golden-brown eyelids with khol until they were as black as the hair. She painted the vermilion dot, the bindi which is the third eye for the use of the soul, in the middle of the smooth brown forehead.

Awkwardly, heaving the flaccid body this way and that, they wrapped the girl in a pink sari. They decked her with a narrow gold necklet, half a dozen bracelets, three rings, gold nose-jewel, and one anklet. They wound a veil, finally, round her shoulders and head and across her face.

Sheelah sighed. She belched softly. She settled herself, like a muslin-bandaged buffalo, back among her cushions on the floor. The Moon relit her half-smoked hookah.

The Moon called the men back into the room.

Sheelah said, "I will give you, for a small additional payment, a jar of the colour for the hair. It should be used once every nine days. Use this green cloth, which I will also sell you, and no other."

"The fingernails?"

"It will serve also for the fingernails. Let her sleep now. She will wake in an hour, perhaps two hours. She will be confused and slow, but she will be awake. Be patient with her. She will not know where she is or who she is."

"We will be patient. Do you wish me to buy the gold things?"

"No. I lend them to you. I know you will return them because I know you are an honourable man."

"That is true, Sheelah," said another of the men. "But—is it permitted to ask—*how* do you know that Feringhia is a completely honest man?"

"Because I am what I am. Because I can see without eyes what those with eyes cannot see. Also because . . ."

Feringhia smiled. He said, "Also because you know that I know that you are a very dangerous woman. I would neither step on your shadow, nor fail to return to you that which is yours."

The Moon lit another hookah and brought mouthpieces. The men—the seeming poor farmers from the desert—thanked her with far greater courtesy than did the bankers and merchants for whom she usually performed such a service.

They settled down to wait for the girl to wake up.

Five

Her first awareness was of a sweet, heavy smell, an atmosphere thick with incense and tobacco.

Then she opened her eyes.

She was in an unfamiliar place, a dark room with shuttered windows. The people in the room were unfamiliar. She did not know where she was. She did not know who she was. The people—four men and an old fat woman—were dark skinned. She glanced at her own bare arms. They were of the same colour. She was one of them. Her instinct dimly told her that the people were foreign, but they were her own people.

She was dark skinned. She was Indian. Soon she would know more, she would remember.

The fat old woman ignored her, but the four men saw that she was awake. They looked at her with kindly, serious faces. The tallest smiled. His face stirred a memory. She knew him. He was a big man, much bigger than the other three, heavy-featured but handsome, with thick silvery hair. She smiled sleepily back at the man, grateful for a link with people, for a door out of the confused darkness of her mind.

The tall man said in English, softly, "How are you feeling, Veena?"

Veena? Was that her name? Why not?

"All right," she said.

"You slept very well, I think."

"Did I?"

"Very deeply, and for a long time. It was good that you slept. You have been sick, you know. I was worried for you. I think you are now better, and soon you will be strong."

His voice and face were kind. Veena thought she was lucky to have such a friend.

Distressed, she said, "I'm very sorry, but I don't know who you are or who I am."

"You are Veena. I am Kashi, called also Feringhia."

"Kashi. Oh yes."

"This is Lal Chand, Ranjit, Sanghavi. And that is Sheelah."

"Oh yes."

"We are talking in English because, as you remember, you do not know your own language very well."

"Don't I? I don't remember."

"We will put that right. Also your memory, we will put that right. You have been *very* sick, you know. But you will be all better when we get home."

"Where is home?"

"A long way from here, a much better place. Everything will come back to you. You will at last take your place in your own world."

"My place . . ."

"As my wife."

"I'm your wife?"

"Not yet. We are affianced." Kashi smiled. "I hoped you would remember at least that, Veena my dear. I am quite hurt that you have forgotten."

"I'm sorry."

"You will stay here and rest for a short time to recover your strength. A day or two, no more. Sheelah will look after you. Sanghavi here will also be always within call."

"All right."

"I have some things to do, some important business. Then we will go home."

Ishur Ghose sat in a cane chair in his own apartment. The sitting-room was airy, sparsely furnished, lined with books.

"I am desolated, truly very sorry, to leave you at such a juncture," he said to Sandro. "But I am absolutely obliged to go to Ghazipur and then on to Benares. A relative in Ghazipur is sick and duty requires me to visit her. And in Benares—"

"Yes?" asked Sandro dully.

"I have been feeling my arthritis quite severely in the last few days. Doctors are no manner of help. Gunga has helped me before and she will do so again. I am a freethinker, but when I suffer from my arthritis I am not *such* a freethinker."

Ishur Ghose knocked out his pipe, a heavy English briar which he smoked in precise imitation of the British officers under whom he had served. He brushed a flake of tobacco off his white homespun trousers.

"This stuff," he murmured, "does attract the dirt. You know what it is? Khadi, exclusively of Indian growth and manufacture. A whim of Ghandi's, the grand idea being to boycott importations from Britain. That dreadful Congress Party wore it as a kind of uniform. I wear it as protective colouring. It makes for a quiet life."

"It does not go well with that English pipe," said Sandro.

Ishur Ghose laughed gently. He said, "I bought this pipe in the Strand, in 1937. I smoke it only in the privacy of this apartment. You know what I like about it? The ritual. I am a terrible ritualist. I fill it from this pouch, in M.C.C. colours to which I am *not* entitled. I strike the match on the outside of this ashtray, and when it is lit I tamp it down with this ingenious metal instrument. All English, all purchased in the Strand in 1937. In my ritual I relive the years when I was active and useful. I feel quite the European."

He laughed again, self-deprecatingly. No one could have looked less European, and he knew it. He was laughing at himself. Sandro felt strong affection and respect for the old man; whatever happened in the next few days and weeks, Ishur Ghose's friendship was a priceless bonus.

Ishur Ghose said, "I think there may be a value in my taking a journey, any journey, at such a time. I may see or hear something. I cannot imagine what, but it was, after all, my profession for many years to keep my eyes and ears open. If there is anything to sniff, my nose is the right shape for sniffing it. It is a highly-trained nasal organ, you know, very sensitive to trouble and to bad smells of all kinds."

"And we wait."

"I do not see what else you can do but wait, in case somebody makes contact. I do not, in honesty, believe that Lady Jennifer was kidnapped for a ransom, but as long as it is possible to believe so then you must wait near a telephone."

Sandro nodded. Colly was waiting near his cousin's telephone at that moment, and would continue to do so until Sandro relieved him. It was unendurable, but it was the only thing to do.

The disappearance, under sinister circumstances, of any British visitor would have caused consternation, and occasioned some police activity. But the visitor who had disappeared was the daughter of a rich and well known nobleman, once a member of the British government, holder of senior military rank; Lady Jennifer herself had many influential friends, not least the conte Alessandro di Ganzarello. It was impossible to play down the event, to keep it out of the world's press.

Representations in the strongest terms were made by the British Embassy. They were scarcely needed. There was a massive police effort to find her, in which newspapers of every political complexion joined. Munificent rewards were offered, officially and privately, for information which would lead to her rescue. Horoscopes, omens, fortune-tellers were consulted. A torrent of misleading information poured into police stations and newspaper offices, as a result of which thousands of fruitless searches were made.

A witch called Sheelah, who lived in a house of ill repute in a tortuous back street in Ghazipur, did very well out of the business. Her comely young acolyte stared, in trance, at the ink-pool, told tea-leaves, and set out a pack of cards so black with grease that the pips and pictures were almost illegible. Sheelah chirruped in her little girl's voice that the missing lady was, without question, in the far south, somewhere beyond Madras, held in a house near the sea on the Coromandel Coast. A senior police officer and a distinguished reporter paid heavily and separately for this information.

"Am I doing you the honour to address the Europe count?" asked a smooth voice at the level of Sandro's waist.

Sandro turned away from the shop window into which he had been sightlessly staring. He glanced down.

The speaker was a little fat Bengali, clean-shaven and slick-haired, middle aged; he wore a neat, inexpensive European suit, a collar and tie, and little pointed shoes. The only element of his dress which removed him from the streets of any European city was that he wore the tails of his shirt outside his trousers; the untucked shirt gave him the air of a man who had narrowly avoided being taken in adultery.

He went on, "Forgive my interruption of the trains of your thoughts. My name is Mister Mohendra Lal Dutt. I think our esteemed mutal, Mister Ishur Ghose, has spoken about me? No? Be that as may, I am bearer of urgent communication from Mister Ghose. You will join me in a cup of coffee? You will be my guest. Any friend of Mister Ghose. He has given me something to show you, to establish all my bona fides, and I am not wishful to wave same in the public eyes."

Sandro allowed himself to be steered into a coffee-shop, a dark place of roaring espresso machines very unlike those of the bars of Rome or Milan. He sat on a rickety chair facing Mohendra Lal Dutt across a rickety table. The Bengali's little pointed toes barely touched the floor when he sat down.

Sandro could not prevent an infant hope flaring into precarious life inside him. Why a message? Why urgent? Why in this furtive way?

Mohendra Lal Dutt ordered coffee. When the waiter had gone away he tugged an oilskin tobacco-pouch out of the pocket of his skimpy, respectable little coat. It was garish and distinctive, broad stripes of red and yellow; it was Ishur Ghose's pouch, his precious echo of England, bought in London in 1937.

"You know," said Mohendra Lal Dutt, "that I could not have this sack in my possessions unless Mister Ghose gave it to me as evidence of authentic communications. It is damn well the ark of the coven to him. I have just come from him at Varanasi, Benares.

He would have given you some rings of the telephone, but the walls have lots of ears in Varanasi. He requested me to inform you that he has found something out. He must see you the face to face at once, the day after tomorrow. You must take the train tomorrow night, the Amritsar Mail. It departures at platform number eight at Howrah Station at seven pip emma. You will be leaping from the train at Mughal Serai in the morning early light. Mister Ghose will be there to meet you, I think. You and the other gentleman will both go, of course? I am thinking Mister Ghose expects you both on the train."

He had nothing to add to this message. He said he knew no more. He insisted on paying the two rupees asked for the coffee, which to Sandro seemed grossly expensive.

"Tobacco pouch?" said Colly. "I never saw the old boy smoke a pipe."

"No. He smokes it only in his apartment. It is to be English, and he does that only in his own home."

"*Then why did he take his pouch to Benares?*"

"Ah. Why?"

"It's possible he couldn't telephone, but why not write? Why not send a letter with the little fat guy you met? Why do we have to go hear the news from his own lips? If we do have to go, why on a goddam train, and why that particular train? Why not fly?"

"Well, why not?"

"Because this thing stinks, chum. Your fat friend stole Ishur Ghose's tobacco pouch to make himself into an accredited messenger. If we get on that train something weird is going to happen."

"Yes, maybe. So we must go on it."

"I'll buy that. *But* he knows you and not me. *And*

somebody has to stay by this telephone, and it's your turn."

"I do not like you going off by yourself on that train, *caro*."

"I do. I'm bored with sitting here being looked at with huge soulful eyes by Cousin Eleanor. Besides, I won't look like this."

"Ah. Now this journey becomes more amusing. I want to come with you. But you are right, I think. He knows me."

"And you're pretty hard to disguise, especially in a country where the average guy is five foot tall."

"And there is this *telefono*."

"There sure is."

"Do you have what you need? You will be what? A Lutheran missionary from Sweden?"

"I have most things, and I'm not going to be any goddam Swede. My old black wig is in my grip like always. It started as the hair of a Mexican Indian, but I don't believe the difference will notice. Skin is no problem. They come all colours here from black to paler than you, so something in my little box will look just fine. Black contact lenses I have. One of Cousin John's guys in a warehouse or someplace can fit me up with some clothes with the authentic smell. I guess I only need an old bedsheet and a pair of sandals. I'll get somebody to show me how they drape —I don't want to cause a scandal by losing my pants on the depot platform."

"You cannot get by, *cretino*. Your Urdu is not good enough."

"Oh yes it is, the way I'm gonna talk it. Remember how Jenny made out one time when she was pretending to be a German when she spoke very little German? She stammered. She could hardly get a word out. It fooled everybody completely."

"*Va bene*. What will you be?"

"Do I have to be anything? Why not just a simple guy going from point A to point B?"

"Everybody in this country is something. Everybody has a caste and a trade."

"Okay. Let's think. I want to be something a little odd, in case I'm a little odd myself, which I'm apt to be. But not absolutely bizarre, to attract a lot of attention. I'll prowl around the bazaar in the morning and grab some ideas."

Colly knew that a sustained attempt at impersonating an Indian, any kind of Indian, was beyond him. But this attempt would not be sustained: it was a few hours in a dark and crowded train. And he had used every waking minute of every day to observe and remember. He had seen how different men walked barefoot or in their sandals, how they wore their clothes and turbans, greeted each other, begged, gave alms or refused to give them, squatted on the ground, lit and smoked cigarettes, spat, urinated in public places, drank water, washed under the hydrants, stood waiting in line or refused to stand waiting in line. He had seen how they worshipped in various temples, treated inferiors and superiors, ate, slept on the ground. He thought that, properly disguised, and with a specific role and category, he could disappear into an Indian crowd for one night on a train.

He took a taxi into the centre of Calcutta in the morning. He looked at the beggars on the street, each of whom, like stallholders in a well-regulated market, had a defined area of the sidewalk; and at the money-changers, of whom there were in some streets as many as beggars, and who called and importuned and plucked at sleeves with even greater determination. Near the New Market there was a rash of tobacconists' booths. Colly stared without seeming to at booth after booth, looking at the customers. From them came a heavy smell of rough local tobacco, and the different smell of pieces of string kept smouldering in the booths, which, like the gas-jets in old-fashioned London clubs, lit the cigarettes of the customers, saving them the expense of matches. The saving of the price of one match was significant to the people of Calcutta. Colly noted this and remembered it: prodigality with matches would brand him an impostor as surely as eating with his left hand.

The Market was a warren of covered alleys, smelling of incense and sugary cakes and cheap cigarettes and cheaper scent. It was very crowded. The men wore dhotis like Mahatma Gandhi, or pyjamas, or approximations of European dress; a saddhu wore only ash and cowdung; a thin, dark-skinned man with a beatific expression wore only a thin digger impaling his foreskin.

Some disguises, thought Colly, would remain beyond him.

He saw a man he took to be a musician, squatting disconsolately in a corner, with a sitar propped against the wall beside him. One of the musician's arms was wrapped in a mountainous, filthy bandage. He could not play his sitar. Yet he was not expected to do or to be anything other than a sitar-player. As a travelling musician, a sort of mountebank, he would be an outsider wherever he went, an oddity expected to be odd, whose oddness would occasion no surprise.

For a night it would do. For one night in a crowded train it was perfect.

Colly studied the glum musician minutely, without seeming to do so. He noted and remembered every detail of his clothes, hair, colouring, the state of his hands and fingernails, the gesture with which he protected, with his good arm, his sitar from the feet of anyone who came too near it.

Colly wore a collarless cotton shirt, with long old-fashioned flapping tails, moderately clean, smelling slightly but unmistakably of bhang, Indian hemp. On his legs were pyjama trousers, striped pink and dirty white, some inches too short but amply cut about the waist and rump. On his feet were cheap plastic sandals. His skin was the colour of coffee with a little milk, darker where the sun had struck. His hair was very black and straight, greasy, growing low on the forehead. His eyebrows were heavy, almost beetling; there were dark tragic shadows below his eyes. The eyes themselves were black. The features were not distinctive. He simply had a face, an ordinary unmemorable dark face, adequately fed but not plump, at which nobody would look twice.

He came from a village near Bikaner, in the great Northern Desert. He spoke Urdu with an appalling stutter. His arm was injured as a result of falling off the outside of a bus in Calcutta, a common mishap, of which came extensive bruising of lurid colour, over which was wrapped a grubby bandage. He knew which overfilled bus he had been clinging onto, and in which street he had fallen off it. But he stammered in talking of this so badly that it was impossible to assess his accent and only just possible to divine his meaning.

In the early evening he walked a long way to the Howrah Station. He had a little money, some betel-nuts and pan-leaves in a cheap brass box, and a battered sitar wrapped in a red cloth.

The station was full of beggars. Many poor passengers were asleep on the narrow segments of the platform allowed them by all the others; the platform looked like an immense array of piles of old clothes spread out to dry or to be inspected for vermin. The smell of the east was pungent. After a long period of waiting, and then a long period of stammering and pointing, Colly successfully bought a third class ticket to Mughal Serai. His stammer attracted some notice, some tutting sympathy, a little laughter. He edged away from the ticket window. He subsided onto the gravity, sweating, crowded platform and settled himself to wait. He had a long time to wait. He looked and listened. Imprinted on his mind was Sandro's description of Mohendra Lal Dutt.

The crowd rose from the platform like a multicoloured wave and rushed to board the train. Colly, rising too, was carried towards a coach. Men of all kinds were fighting their way into the coach, but for some reason there were no women among them. Women were travelling; there had been plenty on the platform, squatting like hens among their bundles. But somehow they were being diverted onto other coaches. It was almost as though a squad of men, chance-met strangers of widely different types, were combining to keep women out of this coach. They were jammed in a knot in the door, crying that there was no room inside: yet men climbed through and found a few inches of room.

One of the men was a little fat Bengali, cleanshaven and with neat, oily hair.

Six

The third-class carriage was desperately crowded with
men of all kinds who lay or squatted or sat in whatever inches of space they could secure. Colly was
jammed next to a fat Sikh, returning all the way to
Ludhiana. Some of the passengers had no luggage
at all, some apparently all their worldly possessions
done up in bundles and tin boxes. To a large extent
the travellers ignored each other, like those in a
rush-hour subway in a western city. But they were
gentler and more tolerant than western commuters.
Colly had no need to be alarmed for the safety of
his sitar; it would not be trodden on. At the same
time the passengers accepted their acute discomfort
with fatalistic tranquillity; they went to sleep, with
placid faces, in positions in which a European would
have found sleep impossible. Colly found that he could
not sink himself that far into his role. Nor did he
want to; nor would he have dared to.

Beyond the Sikh squatted another traveller far from
home, a Hindu from Patiala, and jammed against
him a man from Shahabad. The latter was unusually
friendly and extrovert; soon the three were chatting.
Colly understood a little of their conversation, which
was about themselves. The Sikh was a bus-driver, the
Patialan a potter who made the little earthenware
drinking-cups which are broken after use to prevent

the defilement of one caste by the mouth of another, and the man from Shahabad a coppersmith.

A little way off on the floor of the carriage squatted a little fat ingratiating Bengali. Colly, inspecting him out of the corners of his eyes, was sure that this was the man with Ishur Ghose's tobacco-pouch, although he was now dressed in checked cotton trousers and a skimpy green shirt.

The train thundered north-westwards across West Bengal, which was spangled with the fires of innumerable villages as the evening drew in. Stations came and went, briefly punctuating the rush of the train, and for its great noise substituting a shriller noise of their own. They were like caverns, dark and full of people. Signs in English, Urdu and Bengali forbade spitting and urinating; they were widely ignored. Tea-sellers wailed along the platform; hot-water sellers, for travellers with their own teapots, wailing contrapuntally among them. Coolies tottered under mountainous bundles of baggage. Beggars crawled or sidled the length of the train; an aged woman, grey-skinned and toothless, piped over and over again that she had no father and no mother. At each stop, passengers spilled out onto the platform to buy food. The carriage filled with the smells of curries and of the cheap cigarettes called bidis. The floor became mottled with spittle, red from the juice of pan-leaves.

When the train stopped at a place called Bhagalpur, the little Bengali bounced to his feet like a rubber ball. Colly watched him through eyes that appeared closed. The Bengali made a sign to another man, stringy, almost black, who wore tattered shorts and a kind of night-shirt. They climbed out of the train together. Colly opened his eyes, yawned, stretched, spat, got stiffly to his feet, and followed them onto the teeming platform. He carried his sitar in his unbandaged hand.

The Bengali and his gaunt companion were walking the length of the train, looking into each window. They did so skilfully, apparently casually, giving no appearance of a methodical search.

Colly had seen enough. He climbed aboard the train and wriggled to his place. His body was sprawled and his eyes half-closed long before the men returned. When they did so, the gaunt man's face showed no expression but the Bengali was frowning.

Two or three hours later (Colly had left an exact sense of time far behind with his European clothes) the train stopped at Patna. Most of the passengers got out and joined the shifting mob on the dark platform. A man bought chappatis and tea. Colly, observing and listening, copied him exactly. He paid a few annas. The vendor hardly looked at him. He headed back towards the train. It was almost leaving. Whistles were importantly blown and flags waved, and the shouts of officials and of travellers filled the high dark vault of the station.

Colly did not understand what happened next.

A kind of gentle stampede of ragged brown bodies, chattering in various languages, surged to the train. Colly was somehow carried by a section of the crowd not to his previous coach but to the next one. He had no sense of being pushed or bullied; the men round him were bland and affable, some a family party, some unknown to each other. But they carried Colly irresistibly to the next coach. He was hoisted, with a press of others, into the coach. It was not as full as the first. There were many women in it. Like Colly, and apparently subjected to the same accident, the potter from Patiala was in the new coach. He did not mind where he was on the train, and there was more room here. He scratched his head, talked to himself equably, and lay down on the floor.

The train started again. It thundered westwards through the night into Uttar Pradesh, over the immense fat plain of the Ganges. It was very hot. Most of the passengers slept.

Women had been kept out of the other coach, tactfully, deliberately. An injured musician and a potter had now been expelled from it, so adroitly that the potter had no idea that he had been expelled. Why? Something was going to happen in the next coach at which women must not be present, nor potters, nor musicians: or perhaps injured men: or perhaps Europeans in disguise.

A memory stirred in Colly's brain. What thief would not rob, what murderer would not kill, a woman, a potter, a musician?

Colly felt intense curiosity about the next coach, about the crazy exclusivity which had somehow been dictated to its occupants. He wanted very badly to watch what went on in there.

After a short time the train stopped at Khagaul. Colly propped his sitar in a corner and with an air of sleepy vagueness got out of the train. The station was comparatively quiet. Most even of the beggars and tea-sellers seemed to be asleep. A few people were getting on and off the train. They talked to each other loudly and incessantly. A man and woman, quarrelling, tried to get into the carriage in which Colly had started the journey. A wall of men made it impossible for them to get through the door. They were told, passionately, that there was no room for a mouse in the carriage, it was jammed, other carriages were available, they could on no account enter this one, it was a physical impossibility. The woman was inclined to argue but the man shrugged and led her to the next coach.

Whatever was happening was still happening, then, or had not yet happened.

Colly slipped into the gap between the two coaches. There was no corridor joining them, only a gigantic coupling. He stood on the coupling, flattening himself against the end of one of the coaches. A little light filtered into his hiding-place from the dim naked bulbs hanging far above from the station roof. He regretted the pale colours of his clothes. A station official, important with uniform and flag and whistle, glanced in his direction. His glance lingered for a moment. Colly was sure the official must have seen him, but he gave no sign of having done so. Perhaps he was too lazy and sleepy to bother with a man travelling with no ticket; perhaps it was not his responsibility but another's, in which it would be beneath his dignity to mix.

The train jerked into motion. The sleepers began to accelerate under Colly's sandalled feet. Gathering speed, the train emerged from the dim-lit vault of the station into the huge hot black night. The air struck hot even when the train began to go fast. Colly clung to the end of the coach, his brain confused by noise and vibration and by the ground rushing by under his feet.

The only way to see into the coach was from the roof. The roof was safe enough. There were no tunnels in this infinity of wet flat rice-paddy. Colly's sandals were no good for climbing. He shook them off, letting them fall on the ground between the wide-gauge rails. He pushed his dirty bandage up his arm, clear of his hand. Barefooted and with both hands free he climbed easily onto the roof of the carriage, frightened only that his wig would blow off in the battering hot air that tried to pluck him from the roof and his clothes from his body.

Gripping small, mysterious projections of metal, he lowered his head and shoulders towards a window. He hung downwards, bent right-angled at the waist, his thighs and loins clamped to the metal roof. The thunder of the train and the battering of the wind confused his senses. Handholds and toeholds were small.

Upside down, clinging, Colly peeped into the carriage.

In John Tucker's house the telephone rang.

Sandro, on his way to bed, grabbed it as he always did, hoping as he continued, hopelessly, to hope.

"I trust I have not disturbed your slumbers, Count," said Ishur Ghose's gentle singsong. "I have had a terrible time getting through, you know. Nothing works as well as it used to. That is why I am making this call later than I would have wished. I am simply telephoning to ask if there is any news? Needless to say I have been thinking about nothing else. I personally have drawn blank, I'm afraid. I have done a certain amount of quiet prying, as I promised, but it has got me nowhere."

Sandro said, "Where is your English tobacco pouch with yellow and red stripes?"

"At home," said Ishur Ghose immediately, in a tone of utmost surprise. "I never use it anywhere else. It is so obtrusively Europe, you know, like my old pipe. Why do you ask about it?"

Sandro told him.

Ishur Ghose said, "Mohendra Lal Dutt is quite an ordinary Bengali name. I expect I have met people of that name, but I do not remember one such as you have described. If he said he was a close friend of mine he lied."

"Could your apartment be burgled?"

"Not easily. I was not born yesterday, and I was trained. But by an expert any place can be burgled. Oh dear. I wonder what else they took. Not that the loss of a few of my household goods is to be weighed against our other loss, your loss. It was clever of you to see through the man's deception. I am so thankful you did. But now I am bound to feel a certain amount of concern for Mr Tucker."

"*Anch'io*. But my small friend did not see him, as far as I know. And you yourself would not recognise him."

"That was a very, very prudent precaution. Let us pray that it has worked. If a freethinker's prayers have any value they are certainly at Mr Tucker's service. I simply do not know what we are up against. I don't know why anybody would want you to travel on that train, or what they could have planned. I cannot begin to guess whether it relates to Lady Jennifer's disappearance."

"Will you meet that train at Mughal Serai?"

"Yes indeed. I devoutly hope that Mr Tucker will see me, even if as you say I shall not see him. Perhaps I will see a small fat man calling himself—what was it?—Mohendra Lal Dutt. Perhaps I shall see something of significance."

"We have maybe learned something of significance," said Sandro.

"Yes. I think we have. I will discuss it with Mr Tucker when I see him."

What Colly saw, hanging upside down on the side of the hurtling coach, sent prickles of fascinated horror running down his spine to the back of his neck.

There were about thirty men in the coach, which was not in fact at all crowded. About eight of the men were lying asleep or squatting drowsily, paying no attention to their surroundings, in the state of suspended animation with which Indians make the intolerable tolerable. The Sikh bus-driver was one of the sleeping men. The other men, twenty or more, were awake and alert. Some squatted near the sleepers. A few were on their feet. Among these were the little fat Bengali, Sandro's acquaintance, and the friendly coppersmith from Shahabad.

All eyes were on the Bengali.

He raised his hand to his mouth, fingers extended. He made a circle of his lips. He lowered his hand, exhaling. He was miming the action of smoking a cigarette.

It was the signal.

Onto each of the eight men who were sleeping or dozing two of the others launched themselves. One of the two grabbed the victim's legs, one his arms. All the seized men were thrown violently over onto their faces. A third man knelt on the shoulders of each victim, holding, each one, a narrow strip of fabric about thirty inches long, striped in pale colours. The fabric was in some way knotted and looped. The strips of fabric were slipped over the heads of the victims by the men kneeling on their shoulders, while the arms and legs were still held by the other men. The victims were strangled. All of them were killed quickly but none instantaneously. If there was any noise it was drowned by the noise of the train. Colly, his senses reeling, saw eyeballs and tongues protrude and dark faces become darker as they were suffused with blood.

As soon as they were dead the bodies were stripped. The clothes were searched quickly but thoroughly.

Money, betel-boxes, a few trinkets and charms, a watch or two, were placed in a pile on the floor of the coach at the feet of the little Bengali.

All the bundles and baggage of the dead men were searched. Very little was found which interested the searchers: a pair of shoes, a couple of shirts, a small radio, some packets of cigarettes, a water-bottle in a canvas cover, some religious statuettes, a few other items of small value were added to the pile.

It was all barely worth stealing. All the booty from eight murders made a sad little pile worth a few rupees. It was unthinkably out of proportion, if theft was the main motive of the murders.

Immediately the search was finished, the killers unfolded sheets and rugs and laid them out on the floor. The eight bodies were folded up and wrapped in the sheets. The new, awkward bundles were tied round with cords or with other sheets.

The little Bengali wrapped the whole of the booty in a shirt, knotting the sleeves of the shirt to secure it.

Within a short time the carriage was entirely peaceful and innocent. There were eight fewer travellers. Those that remained squatted or sprawled, peaceful, in a good but not a boisterous humour. Two of them, yawning, pillowed their heads on the bundles which were dead men.

The train made a new noise. Colly, looking down, saw water below, an immense river. He remembered that the train crossed the Son, which joined the Ganges from the south just below the junction of Ganges and Ghaghara. It was a very long bridge. The smooth ink-black water seemed to throw back echoes of the train between the trestles of the bridge, seemed to make an appalled commentary on the murder of eight men for a handful of rupees.

There was no more to see in the coach. It was finished.

Colly hauled himself back onto the roof. Blood pounded through his head from the position he had been in, and his mind reeled with what he had seen.

Everything was now explained. The 900 disappearances were explained.

Colly knew what he had witnessed. He remembered vivid, impressionistic Victorian drawings in a book, a sensational novel founded on historical fact. The murders he had watched were the murders in that book—the limb-holders clinging to arms and legs, the strangler with the narrow handkerchief. The book was *The Confessions of a Thug*.

The train was over the enormous bridge. After a minute it began to slow for the next station. From the map Colly remembered the name Arrah.

What he did depended on what they did. As long as they stayed on the train, heads peacefully pillowed on the bodies of their victims, he must stay on it. When they left it he must leave it, follow, see how and where they disposed of the bodies.

Soon they and their like would have killed 1000 people.

Was Jenny among them? Had her legs and arms been held while the pale scarf, knotted and looped, went round her dear neck, and tightened and twisted until she was dead? Had that happened?

No women had disappeared. But Jenny had disappeared. It was necessary to know more, much more, as much as possible. But it was necessary not to be killed, or Sandro would never know what he knew and Jenny would not be found.

The train slowed to ten m.p.h. and to seven and to a walking pace. It heaved itself thunderously into the station.

Colly prepared to climb down off the roof of the coach onto the coupling. He must be ready to follow if the men left the train.

Brakes screeched. The train juddered to a halt. Immediately one of the men from the coach below was out onto the platform. Two others joined him. They were alert and on their guard, though they would not have looked alert to any casual eye. They glanced all round them all the time. One stood by the end of the coach. Colly, leaning down from the roof, could have touched the top of his head.

Colly could not climb down at this end of the coach without the man hearing and seeing him. He could not jump on him without being seen by the other watchers. If the man saw him he would see that the bandage was a fraud. He would know that Colly had been on the roof. He would know he was a spy. There were more than twenty of them. The Bengali was small and fat but many of the others were lithe, active, tough-looking. Colly might slide down fast and run, but the odds would be heavily against him. If he got away he would not be able to follow and watch the men. If he was caught he would be killed: must be: and Sandro would never know how and Jenny would still be lost.

Colly crawled to the other end of the coach. He was not completely out of sight of people on the platform but it was fairly dark and he did not think he was seen. As he crawled he was aware of movement below him. The twenty men and their baggage were going out onto the platform.

Colly prepared to climb down at the other end of the coach. A man stood there. It was the man from Shahabad who said he was a coppersmith. Colly had seen him strangle the Sikh bus-driver, with whom he had struck up a friendship. He was alert and watchful, a look-out.

There was no way Colly could get down from the roof of the coach.

Should he yell for the police? Shout in English or his inadequate Urdu that eight dead bodies were in the bundles on the platform below him? He would be outshouted by the twenty men. Three or four would climb up at each end of the coach. There would be a great shouting, drowning his voice, that he was a madman, a criminal, about to hurl himself off the roof, to commit suicide. They would struggle with him, pretending to an indifferent crowd that they were trying to save his life. He would get a knife between the ribs, or take a dive head-first onto the platform.

Worst of all they would be warned. They would go after Sandro and get him. If they or their friends had Jenny, she would be buried deeper than a jewel under a mountain.

He was helpless.

"Mukherjee has made a mistake."

"The *feringhi* are not on the train?" asked the big man with the mane of silvering hair.

"The Italian is not. He is safe in Calcutta, in Alipur. The American is on the train. Mukherjee may not see him. I suppose he is dressed up in some way. I did not expect that. Perhaps they are good at disguises, perhaps even as good as we are. I did not expect that at all."

"They will look for my bride. They will not find her but they may be a nuisance while they search."

"Yes. They are cleverer than we thought. That is why they saw through Mukherjee's story, which I expected them to believe. They have powerful friends, also."

"So have you, Ishur Ghose."

"Yes. The same friends. The best thing will be to kill the American here. That will bring the Italian. We kill him here also. It will be much easier to kill them separately than together, I think."

The train started again.

Colly, helpless on the roof of the coach, saw twenty men crossing the platform with many bundles, heavy and of awkward shape. They were not moving as a single group, but as a number of small groups with no contact between them. Other bundles, carried by other passengers or on the heads of coolies, were as heavy and as awkward. The twenty men were not distinctive in any way. They were on their way out of the station in the early morning, before first light. The bodies would never be found.

Colly left the train at the next station. He waited until full day, until important men in Delhi would be in their offices, and then found a telephone.

Jenny had seen pale scarves in the hands of men who came softly up behind Sandro and himself: pale scarves quickly hidden: in the hands of men who were friends of Ishur Ghose.

Ishur Ghose knew that Jenny was going to Kalighat on the day she disappeared.

Mohendra Lal Dutt, as he called himself, had Ishur Ghose's tobacco-pouch. The easiest way for him to have come by it was from the hand of Ishur Ghose.

Was the old man what he seemed? Could the Ishur Ghose they knew be a ringer, an imposter?

Colly was troubled. He trusted his instinct about

people. His instinct vehemently told him to trust Ishur Ghose. Colly had come to like the old man enormously, as he knew the others did. Their judgement of people—Jenny's especially—was acute and highly trained and most rarely proved wrong. But logic obliged Colly to question his instinct.

Sandro had told him what name to ask for, what code-word to use to identify himself. This was in case of trouble. Maybe there was trouble.

After a long time Colly got the right government office in Delhi; in a very short time, by virtue of name and code-word, he was put through to the right person.

Ishur Ghose was very well known by reputation, pretty well known in person, to Sandro's contact. The latter had seen the old man recently, called on him in his apartment in Calcutta only a few weeks before. He described man and apartment. He recounted the outlines of Ishur Ghose's career, the men he had worked for, the men who had worked for him, the assignments he had been given, his subsequent history, his learned hobby, his English pipe and M.C.C. tobacco-pouch bought in the Strand before the war.

There was no doubt, none, that the old man was what he said he was. He was totally trustworthy. He was not just a good citizen: he was, had been, an outstanding confidential public official. Nor could, possibly, the Ishur Ghose they knew be a masquerader. Comparing notes, Colly and Sandro's contact agreed that they were discussing the same man. Not a double, not a twin, not an actor, however brilliant.

Colly told the official in Delhi that he had just watched a Thug murder and that he thought the 900 disappearances were all Thug murders.

The official thought he was mad and said so.

Colly telephoned Sandro and described what he had seen, speaking Italian, which he did not think any eavesdropper would understand.

Sandro knew about the history of Thuggee because he was a student of criminology. He said the Thugs had been entirely wiped out by the British authorities in the second quarter of the 19th century. But he believed what Colly told him.

Sandro said, "Perhaps different people took Jenny."

"Then why did your small fat friend want us on the train to be killed?"

"I think," said Sandro sadly, "you must not discuss this with Ishur Ghose."

"I had the same idea. I telephoned your friend in Delhi. We talked for a long time. I can safely discuss this and anything else with Ishur Ghose."

"*Va bene.* Then do so. I will stay here until you call for me."

Ishur Ghose's eyes twinkled behind the gold-rimmed spectacles. He said, "A mutual friend in Delhi has just been in touch with me on the telephone."

Colly grinned, embarrassed. He began an explanation.

Ishur Ghose said, "Believe me, Mr Tucker, this does not reduce but increases my respect for you. Of course, given the circumstances, you were right to do exactly as you did. Now tell me exactly what you saw on the train and then we will make a plan. The Count is still in Calcutta? Good. We will make a plan for you first of all."

Seven

"What you describe is *impossible*," said Ishur Ghose. "Of course I know the history of *t'hagee*. It was entirely destroyed by Major Sleeman Sahib and his policemen after 1829. By 1840 it was *entirely* destroyed, so the books say."

"Then what in hell did I see?" asked Colly.

Ishur Ghose shrugged. "If Thugs existed and committed their murders in the years of my service, I would have heard of it. If they had merely been in hiding, waiting, preparing, I think I should have heard of it."

Colly went to the police. He did not mention that he had travelled in disguise—this would have taken too much explaining. Many people in India have a pathological fear and detestation of the C.I.A.—as, except in Calcutta and Kerala, most Indians have of the Chinese—and Colly would certainly have been under suspicion as a spy. The consequences might be long-lasting, disagreeable for Colly, embarrassing for the American Embassy, disastrous for the Tucker interests in India and probably in Burma and Ceylon also, and fatal to the search for Jenny. So he said that, peeping into a carriage window, he had

seen eight men strangled by twenty other men in the
manner of the Thugs.

The police already knew that men had disappeared
from the train. Their non-arrival had been reported
from Benares and other places. To this extent Colly's
story was corroborated.

But the Thug part was not believed at all. It was
treated with incredulous contempt. Everybody, every
child, knew that the Thugs had been totally destroyed more than a century ago. The police were
adamant about this. There was nothing to be gained
by pressing the point.

It was, in fact, a mistake to have mentioned it,
though Colly had felt bound to give the police an
exact account of what he saw. His story made it impossible for the police to take him seriously, and
they would not answer questions he wanted answered.
He had to invoke the oracle in Delhi, which took
a long time.

"He travelled as a *musician*?" asked the big handsome man with the mane of silvering hair.

"Yes. An appalling mischance. Of course Mukherjee let him alone, as well as one other who was in
one of the forbidden categories, a potter or dancing-
master or religious beggar . . ."

"This time there must be no mistake."

"We will make sure that there is not. I will arrange
for the American to go in his new disguise, which
I will describe to you, to the temple at Bindachun.
You will arrange for three men of your choice to be
there and to look well at him. They will meet at
the Pilgrim House at night."

"The Pilgrim House again?"

"Yes. It is ideal, and also sanctified by Kali."

* * *

When, at last, the police were told that they could speak freely to Colly, they did so with reluctance and an ill grace.

Colly thought at first that this was local resentment of central authority; or resentment at an inquisitive foreigner. But after a long and weary morning he realised that it was embarrassment. The police had been severely criticised for expensive and repeated failure; it was not their favourite subject for discussion.

Colly discovered that the Ganges plain from Patna to Allahabad had a greatly disproportionate record of disappearances—almost half the total of all those reported in all parts of India in the six months of the disappearances. Every police headquarters had mounds of information, fat dossiers on almost every man who had disappeared. There were a few more descriptions of men seen travelling with men who had disappeared. They were unhelpful and conflicting. There was not the slightest chance that anyone would be arrested on the basis of these descriptions, and only a thin chance that anyone would be recognised.

"Even if," said an Inspector to Colly, "we were able to identify positively a person who was in company of a person reported missing, what could he be charged with? He would say—'Yes, I was travelling on that train on that day, I was in the fourth carriage. I do remember a fat Sikh in a pink turban. He disappeared? I did not know. I supposed he descended from the train at a station. I do not know which station. I did not see him descend. I was, I suppose, asleep when he descended.' What do we do when he says these things, which may be true? This is not a police state but a democratic country with strict laws and strict control of the executive arms. I cannot hold a suspect without a charge. I cannot make a charge with evidence. I cannot fabricate evidence. We do not torture prisoners. What do we do?"

The Inspector spread plump hands in a gesture of despair. Colly nodded. He was not impressed with the Inspector, but the unfortunate man was giving a realistic account of the situation which was also a deeply pessimistic one.

The police had, for some weeks, been taking an obvious and sensible step. They had put plain-clothes men on trains and buses from which disappearances had repeatedly occurred. There were certain other places which had come up more than once in the reports: wayside stations, bus-stops, wells, a road approaching a certain mosque, and above all a pilgrims' hostel near the temple of Kali at Bindachun. At some expense and inconvenience, plain-clothes men had been stationed in these places, in good disguise and with good cover.

"And your men have seen . . .?" asked Colly, knowing the answer.

"Nothing."

"Nobody has disappeared from any place your men have been watching?"

"No person has disappeared. Or my men have disappeared."

"Oh hell."

"It is a problematic situation. If our man has been murdered in the course of duty, his widow is entitled to the appropriate pension. But we do not know that any have been murdered. We do not know anything at all."

"There's a tip-off," said Colly.

"I beg your pardon?"

"Someone has told someone about your stake-outs."

"You are making the allegation that there is treachery within the police? That is a rude and unacceptable suggestion. You will very kindly withdraw it at once."

"I'm sorry, Inspector. I take it back, with apologies. But . . ."

"The thought has entered my own mind," admitted the Inspector heavily. "It has spoiled my beauty sleep. I know and trust all my men, but . . ."

"How many people would know if you posted a particular detective to a bus-stop outside a village in this district?"

"Too many. There are regulations. If a man goes on detached service, he draws subsistence allowance, which must be indented for on a special form. It is processed by all kinds of clerks. The forms go on file, many copies on many files. We are required to state the purpose of the posting, in order to justify the claim for subsistence allowance. Of course it is called 'highly confidential', but it is difficult to be highly confidential when you are required to justify financial outlay from a tight budget."

Colly suggested, delicately, that the Inspector must operate outside these regulations. The Inspector was gravely shocked.

"In my day," said Ishur Ghose, "we managed things better. Expenditure was not accountable in detail. We never made written reports if we could make verbal reports, except depositions necessary for initiating legal action."

"I feel sorry for the cops," said Colly. "Even though the heat's on them, they have to go through all this stuff about forms in quintuplicate. That kind of thing makes security pretty well impossible. One bad apple among the clerks, and all their plans are blown."

"Yes. I am sorry for the police officers. Especially those who are presumably dead. I am sorry also for Lady Jennifer."

Veena was not sorry for herself. She was well looked after by Sheelah and by twittering girls who came on silent feet into a little room with a curtained arch. She had everything she wanted. It was very little. The thing she most wanted she had: a knowledge of her identity and future. She was Veena. Her future lay with Kashi, who came and saw her when he could and was unfailingly kind and gentle. Also, comfortingly, Sanghavi was always within call, an older man, considerate, soft-spoken, a kind of uncle.

Veena saw no one except Sheelah and a few girls, and Kashi and Sanghavi. She was content. She did not want to see anyone else. She waited in passive contentment for Kashi to tell her what to do next.

"Bindachun?" asked Colly.

"It is a place near Mirzapur. If, by some chance that I do not understand, what you saw on the train was what you think it was, then the Temple of Kali at Bindachun is a place you should also see."

"Why?"

"It was, with Kalighat and one other place, the great shrine of the Thugs. If there are Thugs anywhere in India, then there are Thugs at Bindachun. I do *not* believe it, but since you saw what you saw, you should see that also."

"What will I see?"

"How do I know?"

"Good answer."

"And then you shall go to the Pilgrim House of the Temple."

"Where some plain-clothes policemen disappeared."

"Perhaps this *does* make a little sense. I have never been to the Pilgrim House, but people of all kinds go there, hundreds at a time."

"Should be an easy place to get lost in, for a poor sitar player with a stammer and one arm in a sling."

"I most respectfully urge that you should *not* be a musician this time, Mr Tucker. Not at Pilgrim House. It would make you most conspicuous. Please recall that, if your theory is correct, you are specifically facing the possibility that one or more of the murderers whom you saw, or the friends and allies of those murderers, may be at the Pilgrim House. Fine, that is what we want. Only by following such a lead have we any chance of finding Lady Jennifer. But it does not seem to me that we are dealing with fools. You see my point?"

Colly did see it. He said, "How do you cast me?"

"There is the language problem, not to be solved again as you so ingeniously solved it before. There is the problem of behaviour in small things. You must be partially an outsider, yet a—a feasible pilgrim to Bindachun. Are you by any happy chance a mechanic?"

"Sure, kind of. I can fool around with a wrench under an automobile."

"Ah. That will fit in quite nicely. You were an orphan. Your parents were Punjabi Hindus, massacred during the partition riots. You were a young baby at the time. It is a common story. You were adopted by an American Lutheran mission. So you were brought up in ignorance of your ancestral religion, and of your own language, except the little you remember from early childhood. You speak English in the American fashion, of course. That is not so common in India, but it is not so *very* rare, because of the missionaries. So far so good? You then rejected what they taught you at the mission, because—because they tried to make you eat beef. You knew that this was a great sin. They had tried to make you a Christian, but you were all the time a Hindu at heart. So you relearned Urdu at a school. That is why you speak correctly, with quite a good accent, but not so very quickly, because you need to stop and think. At the same time you relearned your own faith. So far so good? You are on pilgrimage as part of this relearning. But you are *not* a beggar, or any kind of holy man depending on alms. That will not do. You have a little money. You have made it by working on machines. This they taught you at the mission school. Americans love machines, so of course they taught you about machines, about cars, typewriters, radios, pumps."

"I don't know a lot about typewriters," said Colly dubiously. "They didn't come into my life much."

"Maybe coffee-machines. Yes, that is a *good* idea. You repair espresso coffee-machines. We will find you a little bag of tools. Of course you will quite naturally use the American words for the tools and the parts of the machines. This is obvious. It all fits in ever so neatly, I think. I begin to congratulate myself on this little saga. Really it seems to cope with our problems. But of course the proof of the pudding, you know."

"Why am I making a pilgrimage to this particular shrine, though? Isn't there a god in charge of craftsmen and mechanics? Wouldn't I go to him?"

"You come to Kali because you have no mother. You do not truly know who was your mother. There is no record of your family, because they were all killed in Pakistan. Kali is your mother, the only one you have."

"I'd sooner have a she-wolf, or Clytemnestra, or even Cousin Eleanor."

They discussed his wardrobe and his luggage, both extremely scanty. He would need another comprehensive coat of skin-dye, but his wig and contact lenses would do.

For hours, and until the old man was rocking with exhaustion, Colly rehearsed with Ishur Ghose the details of his past and present.

The Temple of Bindachun seemed to Colly far less impressive than the great shrine at Kalighat. It was built of stone, rectangular, with a verandah on all sides rising from a flight of five steps. The roof was flat and its pillars rough. Suave priests allowed anyone into the holy of holies on payment of an offering.

The inner shrine was tiny. Colly, two priests and three pilgrims entered together, and nearly filled the little chamber.

Kali was here called Bhagwan, a name spoken only in reverential whispers. Bhagwan was Kali in her most remorseless aspect. The idol was of black stone, four feet high, standing on a slab of black stone. The whites of her eyes were plates of burnished silver: they glared malevolently across the dark, rough-walled little shrine, giving the strong illusion of sight. From neck to shins the statue was covered in a square red blanket. Her black feet rested on an enormous black rat. Beautifully made garlands festooned the idol, made of marigolds and white jasmine and red pomegranate flowers. Instead of hair, she had more festoons of jasmine flowers. These pretty floral tributes were in extreme contrast to the pitilessness of the Goddess's silver stare, and the black rat under her black feet, and the atmosphere of brooding menace which filled the chamber. Colly thought of the Furies, who were known to the Greeks as the Kindly Ones because their true name was too frightening to use; the garlands on the Goddess were a similar, chilling incongruity.

Colly was allowed only a minute in which to marvel at the Goddess. Worshippers thronged in large numbers below the steps of the verandah. As soon as they were allowed to they poured quickly into the Temple and out again. There was no lingering before the shrine. It was as though, Colly thought, they were paying a duty visit—one that could not be neglected but must not be protracted. There was little hysteria, screaming, twitching: there was no bloody sacrifice. It was utterly unlike the scene at Kalighat. Colly was at once disappointed and relieved.

Then he revised this view. He watched the crowd outside the Temple. His antennae vibrated to the mood of the pilgrims, their passionate sincerity; he caught the raw undercurrent of their adoring terror. The terror was there, the fanatic glee, quite as much as at Kalighat in the splashing blood of the sacrificial goats.

The Thugs murdered as a religious duty, as an act of worship to this obscene Goddess. It was with the hem of her garment that they strangled their victims.

"That is he, watching without seeming to watch."
"Yes. Remember well."
"We shall remember."

Three pilgrims walked slowly, through tremendous midday heat, from the Temple towards the hammocks and shade of the Pilgrim House.

A crow, dusty-plumaged and disreputable, cawed morosely from a dusty tree. The pilgrims looked round sharply. On the other side of the road there was a well, a low-caste well the water of which would have contaminated a Hindu of high caste: but a well, and holding water. A gleam came and went in the pilgrims' eyes. One of them smiled openly. Very slightly the party quickened its pace, as though headed now for a specific objective, a clear and pleasurable duty.

They neared the hostel, in and out of which a stream of people was unhurriedly strolling. A beggar held out a bowl towards the pilgrims. He held the bowl in both hands; the little finger of one hand was cocked outwards, like that of a person drinking tea. The pilgrims stopped. One fumbled for a coin. The beggar spoke to him in a language which was not any one of the known languages of India.

In the secret language Ramasi the beggar said that the mender of machines who was not a mender of machines had come to the Pilgrim House. He was even now inside. What omens had they seen?

A crow had spoken within sight of a well of water. Excellent.

Eight

The Pilgrim House was built round a large courtyard, on three sides of which was a deep verandah. A warren of little rooms, most virtually cells, gave onto the verandah; many were full to overflowing with whole families. In the heat of the day, when Colly arrived, hundreds of pilgrims were asleep on the string hammocks called charpoys. Women whacked their laundry on the stones under the taps in the fourth wall of the courtyard. Some children slept, some raced to and fro with cries like those of small birds. In the cool of the evening people squatted all over the courtyard in chattering groups, preparing simple but strong-smelling food.

Colly found it peaceful, pleasant and friendly. He liked this place. No one had bothered him. The people were not grindingly poor. The whole atmosphere was sharply different from that in the courtyard of the temple of Kali. The people were the same people, but here they were in a different capacity. 'Volatile' —that was a word used by Ishur Ghose to describe his fellow countrymen. One minute, and at a moment's notice, they could be gripped by wild and authentic religious fervour, of the kind that can send a man barefooted and unsinged over red-hot coals: the next minute the fervour could go away as quickly and completely as a Caribbean storm, and the people would want to gossip, and smoke, and have dinner. There was a time and place for everything. Religious ecstasy belonged where and when it was appropriate, before the shrine of Kali, or on the ghats of the sacred Ganges. At the Pilgrim House, in the quiet of the evening, it was left far behind.

There were a few booths on the road between the Pilgrim House and the temple. There, for a few paise, Colly bought chappatis, a bowl of vegetable curry and a lump of hot mashed lentils. It was a normal choice. He spent less than one rupee. He knew all the words required for the various transactions, and pronounced them correctly. He took his supper back to the Pilgrim House; hunkering in the courtyard near his cell, in the gathering dark, he ate it slowly. Hundreds of people were doing the same thing.

Colly was careful to use only his right hand, although it was difficult to tear a piece off a chappati and dip it into the curry with one hand. The left hand was contaminated. Because of the uses to which it was put, it was never allowed to touch food. If Colly had used both hands to tear apart a chappati he would have been identified at once as a stranger, an outsider, an outcaste, a mlechcha: an object of derision and, in this place, of dismay and even horror. To eat in his presence would be, to some of the Hindus, a defilement of awful gravity. So he squatted on the dusty ground, part paved and part baked earth, and scooped up his curry with pieces of chappati. He did not think he was in any way remarkable, in appearance or behaviour.

He did not feel remarkable. Indian life, at this level, seemed infinitely welcoming. Because it contained so much contrast and contradiction, it accommodated every oddity. It was easy to be swallowed up, to identify, to change colour inside as well as out. Colly had felt this on the railway station and he felt it again, more strongly, dangerously strongly. He looked at the pilgrims with tolerant indifference. He was one of them. They were all his brothers. There was nothing strange to be seen. If anything was out of the ordinary, it was because it was written that it should be so. Speculation about anything was profitless, a weariness of the spirit, an impertinence.

Colly lit a bidi and inhaled acrid smoke in sleepy contentment. He felt, like a benison, the soothing spirit of fatalism. He was in the Pilgrim House, therefore he was a pilgrim, therefore he believed. It was no good watching for anything or worrying about anything, because what would happen would happen.

No no no. It was one thing to be a good actor, another to dig a trap for yourself. Colly pulled himself sharply out of the warm, comforting soup of passive acceptance. He was not here to understand, by living it, the ethos of Hinduism: he was here because plain-clothes policemen had been planted in this place and had disappeared.

Two, at an interval of thirteen days.

They were Hindus and local men. They had taken off their khaki uniforms and put on dhotis and sandals, and rumpled their hair, and twisted a few belongings into a small bundle, and joined the crowds of pilgrims. That was all they did, all they needed to do. Yet they, and no others, had disappeared. By all accounts they were loyal, experienced, competent men. They both had families; they would have pensions. It was not to be believed that they had run away. They must have been murdered or abducted. Murder was far more likely than abduction. The reason must be that they were policemen, spies.

They had been planted here because there had

been disappearances, many disappearances, from the Pilgrim House. Many people who had come here had not left. They had nothing much in common. They were all men. They were ordinary people, many quite poor, on pilgrimage to Bindachun. They came from many parts of India, spoke many languages, followed many trades.

They had been murdered in this crowded and public place. When? In the middle of the night. It must be so. How? Silently, by strangling.

Colly had come to look at the pilgrims and the Pilgrim House. He puffed at his acrid bidi and looked. What was he looking for?

Well, what? Something that linked with what he had seen on the train. A face, a mannerism, a pattern of behaviour. He remembered faces—the friendly Punjabi coppersmith, the small fat Bengali. Mannerisms? They gestured, smoked, spat. So did everyone else. They were friendly people, affable, extrovert, unusually so.

Colly looked carefully and thoroughly for the two faces he remembered. They had come from Calcutta to this part of the world. But he did not expect to see them; he did not see them. He saw many good-tempered people murmuring and laughing and calling to each other, but none who was unusually extrovert, none who visibly made friends with a stranger, or insinuated himself into a group.

Children slept, some in the cells, some on charpoys under the stars. Colly himself felt sleepy. Soon he would stretch out in his cell. He would pillow his head on his metal-working tools, which clinked in a seedy, incongruous tartan holdall. He decided to smoke one more cigarette, and to be as sensitive as possible, like a photographic plate or a microphone, to anything peculiar, anything at all.

Three men strolled along beside the verandah, softly but earnestly arguing. They spoke a mixture of Hindi and Rajasthani. Colly understood some of the conversation. They were arguing about the use of chemical fertiliser for wheat. An attempt had been made to teach them to use manure from their cows, but cowdung was too precious for fuel to be squandered on the fields. They came to a halt, and squatted close to Colly on the ground. One glanced at him incuriously.

Colly watched them, without seeming to do so, through the smoke of his bidi. Two were middle-aged, one barely adult. They were farmers, villagers, like the vast majority of Indians. They were a long way from home.

Listening intently, understanding what he could, Colly learned that the young man was the son of the older of the others. The third man was a relative, but not a close one; perhaps a distant connection by marriage; he came from a different village. All three had left their wives and children at home.

In the midst of argument, the young man threw away the butt of his cigarette. It landed within inches of Colly's sandalled foot and lay glowing on the dark ground. The boy's father spoke to him sharply. The boy turned and saw what he had done. He was overcome with confusion and apology. In a rush of words he explained that he had been so deeply concerned with the discussion that he had not seen Colly, nor heeded the direction in which he had tossed his cigarette end. In contrition he offered Colly a bidi. Colly hesitated a moment. It seemed most natural to accept. Colly said in careful Urdu that no harm had been done, his foot had not been injured. Politeness now obliged the farmers to include Colly in their debate. The white powder which the govern-

ment provided—what effect would it have on the
wheat? Was the flour to be considered pure? Colly
said that it was a matter of doubt. Many people asked
the same question. Some held that it was better to
have a smaller yield of pure grain than a heavier
one which contained the government's chemical. But
a hungry child was, perhaps, an answer to this argument.

Colly spoke slowly, as though searching his conscience for an exact account of his views. It enabled
him to find the right words, and to frame his remarks
to use words he knew. They listened with the closest
attention when he explained that he had known some
Americans. The Americans spread white powder on
their wheat. But their example was not to be followed blindly: they were *feringhi,* Christians, eaters
of meat and even of beef.

"They are known," said Colly. "To eat pigs."

This was flatly disbelieved. But although the farmers showed plainly that Colly was absurdly credulous,
that he believed and retailed a scurrilous fairy-tale
about the Americans, that he had gone too far in
reporting so unthinkable a defiance of the laws not
only of the Hindus but of Islam also, nevertheless
they continued to treat him with the greatest friendliness. Their manners were perfect. They were very
pleasant men, exceptionally pleasant?

Exceptionally. Bells rang in Colly's head.

He had an excuse now to look closely at the three,
and did so. He did not recognise them at all. They
were very ordinary. He was not in the least sure they
had not been on the train from Calcutta, or among
the party who had carried the heavy bundles off the
train; but he could not tell himself he thought they
had been on the train. He simply did not know, one
way or the other. One—the relative of the father and

son—had a distinctive mannerism: when listening attentively to another who was speaking, he had a way of rubbing his chin with his thumb. It was as though he had a slight, permanent itch on the side of his jaw; as though he had been bitten there, perhaps, by an insect. Colly was sure that if he had seen this mannerism he would have remembered it, because his training and his survival depended on such things. If the mannerism was genuine, this farmer was a stranger to Colly.

But an assumed mannerism is first class disguise. It makes a stranger of a man who is not a stranger. It is the centrepiece of any description of a man who is otherwise unremarkable.

The three had come right up to him from the far side of the compound. There was no reason for them not to do so: but what was the reason for them to do so? They had come and squatted immediately beside Colly. Why not there? But why there? By the simplest and smoothest means—a cigarette end flung in the most natural way by a young man deep in argument—they had included him in their circle, made him their friend.

It was very little to go on. It was nothing. But as far as it went it fitted.

Colly was intensely alert, watching and listening with furious concentration while apparently lazy, sleepy, a little stupid. Without grounds for thinking it, he thought these men were not pukka. They were too flattering, too cozening. They were con-men.

Sandro always said that he trusted *il suo naso*. He sniffed things. Jenny had crazy magic-lantern flashes of feminine intuition, sometimes wildly wrong and sometimes brilliantly right. Colly did not think he was himself naturally intuitive, and in no way psychic or telepathic: but experience had given him a heightened awareness of the phoney, the not-quite-right, of the presence of hostility and danger.

Colly accepted a cigarette, not this time from the young man, but from the man who had a trick of rubbing his chin with his thumb when he was listening to someone talking. Colly smiled his thanks, and lit the untidy little tube of rough tobacco. It was a different kind of bidi from those which he had bought himself at the railway station, and the two which the young man had given him. It was even more powerful in aroma, and hotter to the tongue. The tobacco was very black, coarsely cut, loosely packed. Colly thought it was like a Gauloise which had spent a long time jammed in the trouser pocket of a heavy-sweating truck driver. It was almost more than he could take. He coughed, tried to smile, spat. The cigarette was nauseating.

The man who had given him the cigarette rubbed his chin with his thumb. His chin had grown very large. It was the size of a moon, of a house. The thumb also had grown huge. It was like a banana. The top joint was a mango. It was the trunk of an elephant. Colly's head was swimming. He was himself very small and far away. Concentric circles thrummed out from his head, which was detached from his body.

He coughed again, helplessly. He tried to spit, but the effort was beyond him. He felt a cold sweat breaking out at the edge of his greasy black wig.

He made a huge effort to grab hold of himself mentally. He realised that the cigarette was drugged. He felt angry. Anger cleared his head a little. Drugged, yes. The treacherous bastards. The acrid tobacco hid the taste of the drug. The drug might be any of a dozen. It was very powerful stuff. It was a very fine powder in the tobacco, or the tobacco had been soaked in a solution of it.

The alarm bells in his head had been right. This was danger; these were enemies.

He felt woozy. There was no strength in his limbs. He fought a huge temptation to give in to the languor of the drug, to let befall whatever befell. He wondered if he could stand up and make it to his cell. He wondered what would happen if he got there.

He pretended to smoke the rest of the cigarette. It burned fast because the tobacco was dry and loosely packed. Instead of drawing in the smoke he blew outwards: this made the end of the cigarette glow as though he were inhaling it.

He looked at the three men with a blank, unfocussed eye. He let his mouth fall open and his head wobble on his neck. He dropped the cigarette. It was much easier to pretend to be drugged when he was drugged.

The three men had drawn a little closer to him. They looked at him in silence, expressionlessly. There was no hostility in their faces but there was no friendliness either.

Colly mumbled that he must sleep. He made as if to try to get to his feet. He was sure that he could now have stood up unaided, though not easily, but he pretended that he found it impossible. His brain felt clogged with thick grey smoke and his eyes continually lost focus, but he forced himself to be as much on his guard as possible.

It was quiet in the compound now. A few of the pilgrims were awake and softly talking; most were asleep. The oil lamps and low fires gave a little light. The three could easily kill him now, but they would be lucky to do so unseen. Surely they would let him get to his cell. There, if they planned anything, they could carry out their plan in private. Surely that was how it would be.

He tried again to get to his feet, whimpering at his helplessness, his head lolling. Expressionless, father and son helped him. Each took one of his arms and helped him to his feet. They were much stronger than they looked. They were little men, light-framed, scrawny; but they lifted him effortlessly to his feet. They were neither rough nor gentle, but like indifferent male nurses, briskly competent, bored, doing their jobs.

Erect, Colly badly wanted to test the strength of his legs by putting his weight on them. But he did not do so. If he supported himself, even for a split second, the men holding him up would feel him doing so. They would know that he was less drugged than he seemed. They would know that he had not smoked as much of the cigarette as he pretended, that he had fooled them. They must think that he was hardly conscious, and would pass out the moment he was lying down on the rough piece of carpet in his cell.

Effortlessly, with astonishing strength, father and son walked Colly the few paces on to the verandah and towards his cell. He mumbled incoherently and allowed himself to dribble.

The two men, jammed close to him, reeked of curry and cheap tobacco. The father, on Colly's left, turned to face him for a moment. His face was inches from Colly's face. He gave unpleasant evidence of appalling breath. He seemed not for a long time to have used a chewing-stick to clean his teeth. Colly felt a fogged surprise: devout Hindus are usually meticulous about cleanliness.

Pretending to be helpless, Colly was helpless. Each

of his arms was gripped above the elbow by two thin
and powerful hands. But this cut both ways. Since
father and son were holding his arms, neither had
an arm free. But the third man, the man who rubbed
his chin and carried drugged cigarettes, the man with
a clean, threadbare white singlet and capacious dhoti:
he was walking close behind Colly. Both his hands
were free and he could conceal a scarf in the loose
folds of the dhoti.

It was dark under the verandah. Colly felt his spine
prickle. He felt the breath of the third man on the
base of his own neck.

They supported him to his cell. They knew which
his cell was. How?

They lowered him, neither roughly nor gently but
with indifferent efficiency, on to the strip of ancient
carpet. He went down flaccidly and lay on his face.
It was very dark, but the archway of the cell was a
pale area from the lamps and fires outside.

Colly's right hand flopped, as he intended, on to
the ragged tartan holdall. Its zip was broken. His
hand slid inside the bag to the clumsy, elderly tools
which Ishur Ghose had produced. He curled his fingers, very slowly, round a piece of metal. He could
not tell what it was. His fingers felt fat and numb.
He moved as delicately as possible so as not to make
tool clink metallically against tool. He wanted the big-
gest wrench as a club, but he did not dare to grope
about for the wrench. He must make do with whatever he had got.

He mumbled again. Then he made his breathing
become slow and regular. It was terribly difficult. He
was frightened and excited, in spite of the heavy
effects of the drug, and he wanted to breathe quickly,
to pump his lungs full of oxygen. But quick breathing would show that he was awake, alert.

From tiny sounds he knew that all three men were in the archway of the cell. They were all still there. None had gone away. It was still three against one, or a lookout and two against one. They were waiting until they were sure that he was deep in drugged sleep.

With every second he was in fact more widely awake, more able to think and cope, more confident that his muscles would respond. Adrenaline overcame the drug. His heart was pounding. He was almost suffocated by suspense and excitement, by the presence of a murderous threat a few feet behind him. He lay listening intently, through the noise of his own stertorous breathing, for a movement from the door.

It was perhaps suicidal folly to lie face downwards waiting for an attack. But unless they attacked he would know no more—know nothing except that an apparent Rajasthani farmer carried at least one doped cigarette. There was no way of finding out more except this way. Frightened, excited, listening desperately, motionless, flat on his face, Colly waited for a whisper or a movement.

The smell of the men was overwhelming in the airless little room. It would have been airy but they were blocking the archway. There was a smell of curry and rough tobacco and a rancid smell of bad breath and a smell of wild animals, a smell of blood and carrion.

Colly heard a single whispered syllable.

Before he had time to move he felt his ankles grabbed and held, each by a narrow powerful hand like a claw. At almost the same moment a knee landed on his shoulders, and a split second later he felt a strip of cloth going round his neck.

He made three violent and simultaneous movements. He twisted onto his left side, half throwing off the man on his shoulders; the strip of cloth jerked tight round his neck. Being on his side enabled him to bend his knees. He did so with all his force, and then straightened his legs, pounding with the soles of his feet at the head or chest of whichever was crouched at his feet. At the same time he brought his right hand, gripping the piece of metal, in a back-handed chop at the man who was trying to garotte him.

From the weight of the piece of metal he knew it was the big wrench. It clubbed into some part of the man—arm, shoulder, neck. It did not hit his skull. There was a grunt of pain. Colly felt the piece of cloth relax its throttling pressure round his neck. The man, invisible, tumbled away from Colly. Colly flailed out in the dark with the wrench. He did not hit the man again. At the same time he continued to kick out at the other assailant, who let go of his ankles.

One of them gasped a command. Suddenly they were gone.

He had not killed or disabled any of them. Probably it was just as well. Even though he was trying to do the police's work for them, the police could hardly overlook violent assault in the Pilgrim House. Colly might say it was self-defence, but a dozen witnesses would swear to a berserk, unprovoked attack. His disguise would be pierced, his cover blown. He would be a C.I.A. spy, or an international drug runner. He would be in appalling trouble. He could not drag Ishur Ghose into this; it might be better to keep quiet about Sandro. From the point of view of the company, it might be better not to say anything about John Tucker, to deny all connection. This would leave him horribly on his own. The Embassy in Delhi would be embarrassed and angry.

In the white-hot moment of the fight, he had tried to smash the skull of one man with the big wrench, and kick off the face of the other man. It was a good thing he had failed.

He lit a match and searched the little bare chamber. The three had left nothing behind. There was no blood on the wrench or on the floor or on his own scanty clothes. The only trace of their presence was a lingering, pungent smell.

Would they try again? No—no chance. They wanted to kill silently and unseen. Naturally—who didn't? If they tried again, three or thirty of them, he would shout loud enough to knock the stars out of place. They knew that. He was wide awake, alert, frightened, angry. They knew that too. To try again they would have to take him by surprise, not here but elsewhere, when he felt quite safe.

Obviously the three would not be around at daybreak. They would have slipped away in the dark, far away into some bolthole. There would be no one for Colly to identify.

Colly reasoned that he was perfectly safe for the rest of the night, and could stretch out and go to sleep. But he did not quite believe his own reasoning. He sat in the archway of his cell, his back to the wall, where he could see anybody coming. He smoked too many bidis (his own safe bidis) and stayed awake. The adrenaline drained gradually away, leaving him relaxed and sleepy. He turned the whole thing over and over in his mind. He got nowhere.

Nine

Ishur Ghose listened to Colly's story with the closest attention. He asked him to repeat his description of the two older men and the young one. He wanted to hear all of the conversation about farming which Colly had understood. He was interested in the drugged cigarette. He said he did not believe that the nervous mannerism, of stroking the chin with the thumb while listening, could have been assumed: he himself, he said, would once have been capable of such sophistication of disguise and performance; Mr Tucker and the accomplished Count were doubtless capable of it; but surely not a man who tried to murder a low-caste mechanic for a few rupees.

"These guys were Thugs," said Colly. "You don't accept that, but I do. They wouldn't worry how much money I had, not primarily. But why did they pick on me?"

'There are two possible explanations, Mr Tucker, both of which have undoubtedly occurred to your own keen brain. The first, which I am afraid is the more probable, is; that in some inadvertent fashion you gave yourself away to these men. In a den of thieves that is a dangerous thing to do. A den of murderers, to speak more exactly, as this gurdwara gives every appearance of being. What slip you made, if you made one, is a question about which one can only conjecture. Did you by any chance use your left hand for eating? Europeans are very apt to do so. No? Then it was something else. You looked one hundred percent correct, that I can vouch for."

"My little chums saw I was a phoney, guessed I might be a spy, and took the appropriate action?"

"It is hypothesis number one, don't you agree?"

"Yes, it is, goddam it, but . . . Actually I thought I was pretty good in there. I kept my head down and my nose clean. If I committed some big social gaffe, wouldn't that show on somebody's face? Wouldn't somebody laugh or look shocked or something?"

"That is true. A sharp point. A blunder on the large scale would have been remarked on, visibly and audibly. That I grant you. But you were evidently being watched by hypersensitive eyes, alert for any falsity, any tiny wrong note in your performance, if I can so express myself. But all this is only one hypothesis, and there is another possibility. You said the police told you that many persons have disappeared from the gurdwara, the hostel, in recent months?"

"Yes. I forgot the figure. Quite a few."

"Then your recent acquaintances—Thugs as you believe, simple thieves as I must still believe—have been killing men in that place. A man all on his own is clearly the easiest man to kill. You were one such. You had no wife to scream and make a commotion, no friends to defend you. And you do not look, if you will forgive me the personal observation, a very powerful man. You are not built on the lines of our friend the Count. Perhaps they did *not* see anything wrong in your performance. Perhaps there was nothing wrong. They did not think you were a spy. They simply saw that you were alone, defenceless, friendless, not absolutely without funds, and for these good reasons decided to kill you rather than another."

Colly nodded. Either of these explanations would
do. There was a third: that he had been fingered
as the plain-clothes men had been fingered. The only
person who knew enough to finger him was Ishur
Ghose. And the old man had been checked out to
an extent that made suspecting him impossible.

Colly wondered how he had given himself away.

"I must go home," said the big man with the mane
of silvering hair. "I can delay no longer, for the
sake of my bride if for no other reason. It is not
seemly that she stays any longer in that house."

"You can *not* go yet."

"No. You must get the Italian here. When we have
killed them both we will go."

"The American has not been easy to kill."

"I sent only three men against him. It was not
enough. I shall send twenty men against the two of
them. We must make an end."

Sandro came to Mirzapur at once, at Ishur Ghose's
suggestion. He agreed that Colly was perhaps under
threat, and that the threat was greater if he was
alone.

Ishur Ghose had a telephone number. Any news of
Jenny, any demand for ransom, would be passed on
at once by John Tucker.

"Assume that Pilgrim House is a thieves' kitchen,"
said Colly. "Assume or not that it's a Thugs' kitchen,
Ishur Ghose, but assume anyway that it's a place
where murderers hang out."

"Yes, we must assume so," said Ishur Ghose.

"Then I have to go back there."

"I think not," said Sandro.

"I respectfully concur," said Ishur Ghose. "You would be running your head into a noose, with no useful purpose being served. Your friends must know you tricked them, by most cleverly detecting the drug in the cigarette and pretending to smoke it. Therefore they know you are not what you seem. They know you would recognise them. Therefore they will not show themselves to you. If they are there, they will be more sly. You will not see them. They will make no mistake. If they are not there, you are wasting your time."

"I have plenty of that," said Colly.

"No," said Sandro. "Because all the time people are disappearing."

"Yeah. I take that back. We have to get on. We need to build up a picture of this thing, grab hold of a pattern. We need to look at some more places where a lot of guys went missing. Maybe where some of these plain-clothes cops went missing too. And this time," he turned to Sandro, "I'd just as soon you got off your fat can and joined me, chum."

"Once again I concur," said Ishur Ghose.

Sandro drew a piece of paper out of the pocket of his beautiful silk shirt. He said, "Benares."

"Convenient," said Colly. "Only fifty miles away."

"They have murdered people in Benares?" asked Ishur Ghose, startled.

"Many people. Unless they have all drowned in the Ganges."

"That is dreadful. Really a sort of desecration. I am of course a freethinker, like Pandit Nehru, but I suppose I retain from childhood a feeling that Benares is *the* holy city. It is Jerusalem, you know, or Mecca. Amritsar for the Sikhs. Would I be right in quoting a place called Salt Lake City? I did not know what a Mormon was until I read about Presi-

dent Johnson. I still have some difficulty in understanding. Perhaps we could discuss that at some future date convenient to all parties, Mr Tucker? I am
interested in comparative religion. It is another of
my hobbies. It was of course necessary to my work in
the good old days, as I continue in secret to call them.
The ethnological aspect. There I go, gassing again. I
was saying that to murder someone in Benares is a
pretty caddish trick. But of course, to be brutally
practical, for anyone who wants to do a bit of mur-
dering, it is simply ideal."

"Yeah?"

"Just what the doctor ordered, as they say. Thousands and thousands of strangers, travellers, people
unknown to anybody else in the place. Rich as well as
poor. And of course, for a devout Hindu, it is *the*
place to die. People go there to die. So I suppose, if
a bloke has to be done in, that is where he would
choose to be done in."

"We try to avoid," said Sandro.

In a place with a settled population, in a homo-
geneous context, Sandro was almost impossible to disguise. Before the invention of coloured contact lenses
the impossibility was absolute, because the brilliant
sapphire eyes in the swarthy Latin face were unfor-
gettable. Even black eyed he was extremely distinctive; in an undernourished country like India his
giant frame stood out like a sacred elephant.

But Benares, once and now again called Varanasi,
has a thousand temples and a hundred thousand pilgrims. Almost anything goes, because almost everything is already there. It is a place of pilgrimage for
Buddhists and Jains, as well as for lovers of Shiva
and Hanuman and Ganesh, of Krishnha and Kali
and Mother Gunga herself. It is a place of a thou-

sand languages, physical types, and religious observances.

"We can fit you in all right, Count," said Ishur
Ghose. "But it is a big haystack to go looking for
a needle in. Still, we have something to go on. We
are beginning to get the rough outline of a picture."

Two holy men squatted on a ghat above the Ganges.
They were not together. There was no contact or
communication between them. It was impossible that
there should be any.

One was of very familiar type, a saddhu of one of
the dozens of sects which study yoga and seek perfection and inner understanding by trance, austerity, and
total conquest of the body. This one wore only an
ochre-stained loincloth, intricately twined, and a sort
of skimpy shawl of dirty red cotton. The rest of him
was covered in grey ash. He had a full, straggling
black beard; his hair was long and wild. Round his
neck was a string of beads made of nuts. Little of his
face was visible under the rancid beard and hair; that
little was placid, and the dark red-rimmed eyes were
peaceful and inward-looking.

Given enough of somebody else's hair, thought
Colly, and this disguise was just about the easiest in
the world. You could adopt the lotus position if you
wanted to, but you didn't have to. You didn't have to
act any part, but just sit around and stare into space.
Nobody expected you to talk. Nobody would be surprised at anything you did. You could go where you
wanted, and watch without seeming to watch. Anywhere you went you were part of the scenery.

A few paces away a holy man of totally different
aspect told the heavy, polished beads of a long rosary. He was wrapped in a voluminous robe of rough
woollen material, dirty yellow in colour; a heavy

metal pendant, curiously wrought, hung round his neck; he wore a big flapped hat with a pointed crown, which came down over his ears and hid all his hair. His face was yellow, his eyes narrow and black. He was an enormous man: an overfed lama: doubtless one of the refugees from the rich lamaseries of Tibet which the Chinese and their Cultural Revolution had purged out of Lhasa and the mountains. No doubt he was on pilgrimage to the Deer Park, the garden outside Benares where the Buddha first began his teaching sitting cross-legged under the tree. He was an exotic on the banks of Gunga, but not a totally unfamiliar sight. He might beg for his food, on the excuse that he was allowing people to acquire merit by giving to him—there could be a dozen wooden begging-bowls under his immense robe—but he probably had plenty of money. These outlandish people did.

Sandro was suffocatingly hot in his horse blankets, but otherwise reasonably comfortable. He could and did carry enough hardware for Colly as well as for himself. The skin outside his eyes had been pulled backwards and upwards, and fixed by tiny removable stitches—Ishur Ghose was very clever at the stitches, in spite of his age and his trembling hand—which went far to turning a western face into an eastern. In any case he was frankly a foreigner, and could look foreign. A little bad Hindi and Urdu was all he need speak. He could behave very much as he liked, as long as he retained a grave, graven dignity and avoided looking directly at a woman.

Behind the two holy men a clump of ornate temples soared spikily into the blazing sky. All about them, individuals and groups and large families squatted under wickerwork umbrellas; all their possessions, their cooking pots and clothes, were stacked round them like sandbags against a flood. The huge river below was yellowish-brown, smooth, steadily flowing. Hundreds and hundreds of Hindus were always immersed in it, fully clothed, solemn as owls, praying, having their sins and their skin-diseases washed away by the effluent of a million sewers.

The men who had disappeared from Benares were all visitors, none local. Some whole groups had disappeared, of three and four and even five men; some were thought to have been alone. All were Hindus and on pilgrimage, except two Muslims, father and son, who were visiting a relative who was a weaver of silk brocade. The pickings from some of the murders might have been pretty good; from others it was obviously tiny.

No one could have been murdered on the open spaces of the ghats themselves: but it was there, or in the forecourt of a temple, that an ingratiating stranger was most likely to strike up a conversation. Colly thought that, if he saw it happening, he would recognise it. It would not be simply conversation arising out of propinquity, as in the train: nor the trick of the cigarette-end, as in the Pilgrim House. It might be a dozen things, a hundred; but it would be a recognisable pick-up.

Sandro had seen the other episodes clearly enough through Colly's eyes, and he too knew exactly what he was looking for. It was the easy, natural, self-deprecating style of the free-loader who inserts himself, ever so charmingly, into a high-spending group in a smart bar in Rome; it was the smooth, boyish charm of the gigolo who gives a bored middle-aged lady the evening of her life in a night-club on the Costa del Sol. It was something you could not fail to sniff, if it was there to sniff and you were sniffing for it: but something you might completely miss if you were busy with other things.

The plan was to watch, follow and grab. After the grab, the highly incongruous black Oldsmobile waiting in a garage near a mosque. Then, with Ishur Ghose's help, the interrogation. At some stage, presumably, the police; but these people had men planted in police-forces. They would know what the police knew the moment the police knew it. Which meant that they would change their plans or methods and the police would never know. And in the next six months another 900 people would disappear and Jenny would never be found.

A man in the khaki pants and bush-jacket of the Railway Police was chatting to a Mahratta storekeeper, a traveller, in the station at Kashi. The policeman was a big man; his mane of silvering hair was neatly brushed as befitted his official position.

The men spoke partly in Urdu, partly—low-voiced —in a language which no one else in the station would have understood.

"There is a saddhu," said the Mahratta, "whom you shall recognise by a red shawl and a necklace of which three of the beads are green and two are red and the rest brown."

"Why are you telling me about a saddhu? You know the rule about holy men who are beggars, and beggars who are holy men. It was breaking the ancient rules which brought upon us the great sorrow, from which we have only now been granted relief."

"Jemadar, he is neither a beggar nor a holy man."

"Oho. Stands it thus?"

"There is, secondly, a man very great in height and bulk, a Bhotiya, a seeming guru from Tibet."

"A lama. So?"

"So he is not a beggar. Nor does he come from Bhotiyal. Nor is he poor. If the omens are propitious . . ."

"The omens are continually propitious. It is as though Bhowani were continually thirsting for blood, for unceasing draughts of blood."

"That of those two will be pleasing to Her."

The officer of the Railway Police saw, getting off a train, a Captain in the same service. He moved casually but quickly out of the Captain's sight.

Later he gave to two dozen small, unremarkable men, with friendly and easy manners, such descriptions as he had of the saddhu who was not a saddhu and the lama who did not come from Tibet.

The saddhu, squatting half-tranced on the Dasaswamedh Ghat, raised his voice in gentle incantation. It was not surprising to any of the pious folk on the ghat that so holy a man, privy to internal and external mysteries, should chant in an unknown tongue.

Colly sang in Italian, "A man was looking carefully at my necklace. It has some beads of different colours. It would identify me."

After a pause the immense Buddhist in the huge hairy robes raised his own deep voice. To the click of his beads he intoned a prayer in a tongue which some took to be Chinese, some Tibetan; it occurred to no hearer that it was the same language the holy and half-crazed saddhu had used.

Sandro said, "If he is a friend he is a friend of Ishur Ghose. If he is an enemy he is perhaps still a friend of Ishur Ghose."

"Jeepers, what a thought," chanted Colly in English.

The man who had looked at the beads stood by the high-piled earthenware pots in which the faith-

ful carry away the holy water of the Ganges. He
could see a short way up the narrow street leading
into the town. He could also see, some way away along
the ghat, the two motionless holy men.

He raised his left hand and with it rubbed the
lobe of his right ear.

There was a tiny answering signal from a man who
had nothing to do, who was waiting in the street
with the manner of a beggar too idle to beg. He
glanced at a twelve-year-old boy, and rubbed the
lobe of his right ear with his left hand.

The boy showed no sign of having seen this casual
little gesture. He spat, yawned, and stood up from
the corner where he had been squatting on his heels.
Then he hurried away up the narrow, crowded street
as though suddenly reminded of some task and fear-
ful of a beating.

"*Aspettiamo,*" chanted Sandro liturgically, clicking
the beads of his rosary.

"*Bene. Ma ho paura.*"

"*Anrh'io.*"

Colly was not scared of the present. They were in
full view of hundreds of people under a blazing sun.
But he was scared of the future. It was reasonable
to assume that they, or at least he, had been spotted
by one of a gang of unknown size. Men he had never
seen before would be watching him. It was no longer
any good getting rid of the beads. He and Sandro
must not split up: that would be suicidal folly. But
if they stayed together, even only this much together,
Sandro would be spotted if he had not already been
identified. What to do? Stay put and wait, as Sandro
said. If they moved they learned nothing. If they
kept running away from trouble they would never
learn anything.

But eventually they must move: in the evening, when the tortuous little streets darkened, and shadows filled alleys where a platoon could be strangled without anybody noticing.

Why did his necklace mean something, if it did? Obviously because his hotel room had been searched. Wig, black contact lenses, dhoti, sandals, make-up, all that stuff had been in his room. Hidden, but how can you hide anything in a hotel room from the hotel's own staff?

It figured. The Thugs had spies in the police, they had spies in hotels. Of course they did. All crooks did.

Meanwhile the man who had looked at the necklace was still in sight.

And within his sight, in the narrow street, several small groups of men had gradually and idly assembled.

There were a few pilgrims, a milk-seller, a hawker of bottles of Ganges water, a vendor of Shiva lingas, small phallic symbols in marble, one of bead necklaces like the saddhu's, one of flowers. There was an off-duty bus-driver, two porters from the railway station, and a group of tired workers from a silk-mill. There were three dapper young men in European trousers, messengers or junior clerks, and near them an officer of the Railway Police studying a revised train time-table. In all there were two dozen men; there were also, in an equally idle group, several teen-aged boys.

The narrow street was the only way from the ghat, except by water.

Ten

Kali, Bhowani, was here Durga, and still black, and
wore round her neck a necklace of severed heads, and
round her waist a girdle of severed arms. She was
the subject of hundreds of garish paintings, among
the thousands on sale in the bazaar of Benares for
the faithful to take away and worship—Hanuman the
great merry monkey, Ganesh the still merrier elephant, Rama the Hunter, Vishnu the Preserver,
Krishna the seductive young Lover, all benevolent
and cosy gods, gods of reassurance and comfort, gods
to approach with awe but trustingly. In this genial
pantheon Kali was a dreadful, ever-present exception:
the dark reverse of the coin of Hinduism, worshipped
with blood at Kalighat, inspiring terror, mentioned
in whispers, the stuff of nightmare.

The bazaar had seemed a good place to go. A
saddhu would attract almost no curious attention;
a giant lama would attract attention but no astonish-
ment. There was plenty of light and a ceaseless throng
of people. The trackers must show themselves, because in the crowded alleyways they must stay close.
Colly and Sandro were used to tailing and to being
tailed. They could infallibly spot a tail, if it was the
same man for even a short time, by stopping, starting, slowing, speeding, and observing if anyone behind were doing the same. If different tails took over

from each other in quick succession, and some tailed in front, then it was more difficult to spot them.

They left the ghat, apparently separately but not far apart, under the unconscious protection of two large families. All the members of both families were dripping with Ganges water; it dribbled from their hair and steamed out of their drying clothes. They were burdened with cooking-pots, brass pujah vessels, and with clothes and blankets. They were happy because they knew they were cleansed, sinless. On all known form, the enemy would make no attempt on its enemy under the eyes of women. Nevertheless, the long narrow street, much in deep shadow, was uncomfortable.

As they went into the bazaar, Sandro passed close to Colly. He spoke without moving his lips. He said, ventriloqually, "I keep a few paces behind you."

"That looks after my back. What about yours?"

"I am too prominent to kill suddenly in a crowded place. Even if no women see. Too many people notice me."

"I hope you're right, chum."

"*Anch'io.*"

It might be possible to draw a tail close to them; even, with luck, between them. If these people knew their business at all, the tail would have close support, but it might still be possible, in certain conditions of crowd and of patchy darkness, to grab him and get him to the car in the garage by the mosque.

Colly strutted, storklike, through the teeming, noisy alleys. His eyes appeared to be sightless; at the edge of his vision he was aware of a man close behind Sandro, a too-idle man in dhoti and singlet staring at the defaced remnants of a poster; then of a smooth young clerk lingering pointlessly outside an ivory store with closed shutters, on which a handwritten sign in Urdu directed the customer to another merchant; of a railway coolie with half, but only half, his attention fixed on a stack of sacramental brass pots.

They were ringing the changes very fast. They were professionals, not top-class, but knowing how it was done.

Colly stopped beside a neat, geometrical display of medicinal herbs and roots spread on the sidewalk. The old woman selling the medicines began chattering to him; her tone was wheedling and deeply respectful. Colly understood not a word; he ignored her. He raised his head, and slowly turned completely round, his expression benignly arrogant, as though allowing himself to observe and tolerantly despise the humdrum physical world which he had long left.

Sandro, three yards away, was devoutly clicking his beads. He seemed to be looking uncomprehendingly at a display of coloured powder for making the tilak, the badging mark on the forehead. His slanting black eyes, his yellow skin, his copious robe and bizarre hat, his placid impassivity combined to make him look totally, incredibly oriental; Colly could tell he was Sandro, but he could hardly believe he was not a lama.

Beyond him, close, too close, a labourer looked quickly away as Colly's eyes swept him. The labourer bent his gaze on a vendor of incense-sticks. He glanced once, furtively, at Colly, then immediately looked back at the incense-sticks.

This man was not good at it. Maybe he was a beginner. Maybe he was the one to try for.

Slowly, his expression opaque, Colly walked back the way he had come. He passed close behind Sandro. He smelled, even among the mingled and aromatic smells of the bazaar, the dusty aroma of Sandro's robes. Sandro showed by a small twitch of his shoulders that he knew what Colly was doing. One hand was hidden in the capacious folds of the robe; only one continued to click at the beads. Colly wondered what weapon Sandro was holding in the hidden hand.

The labourer still stared at the incense-sticks. There was something rigid, tense, about his posture. He was a man wondering what was going to happen next.

Colly went on past the labourer. The labourer was between Colly and Sandro. Colly tried to identify, with eyes that pretended to look inwards, the man he knew would be close on the tail of the tail.

Two men looked away quickly; three, four. None was more than a few yards away. Colly had seen none of them before. The others whom he had seen were behind again, dropped back to the rear rank, invisible but close, too many, too close.

They were waiting. Ultimately their chance would come. It must. They were in no hurry. They were making sure. It was cat and mouse: very many cats, two mice.

Colly raised an arm slowly, stiffly upwards, like a saint pointing to his vision in a Flemish primitive painting. A few people glanced at him incuriously. If he had a fit they would let him lie.

In a thin high voice Colly called out, "*Troppo. Non possiamo.*"

He turned again and walked stiffly past the labourer and the gigantic lama. He stopped and looked opaquely back. The labourer had disappeared. In his place another man stood fascinated by incense-sticks, a humble pilgrim.

It was stalemate: but the game had to continue.

Slowly, slowly, Colly and Sandro led the pack of

their pursuers out of the bazaar into the tangle of little streets round the great Golden Temple and, beside it, the white-domed mosque of Alamgir. The alley outside the temple was full of people; pilgrims of all kinds poured in and out of it, flower-petals were trodden in a scented mass on the stones of the alley; well scrubbed Brahmins, alert for tribute and scrupulous about the rules, hovered at the entrance of the temple; it was a safe place; but the game was still stalemated.

Colly squatted at the edge of the alley, near the great archway, on a squashy carpet of jasmine and hibiscus petals which had fallen from the garlands taken inside. Sandro stood not far away, looking with a Buddhist's contemptuous pity at the hordes of ignorant polytheists hurrying to worship their idols. A Brahmin, marked by his brahminical thread and by the knotted tuft of hair in the middle of his shaven pate, accosted him with the mixture of superiority and open greed which, to the Indian poor, identifies all priests. Sandro brushed him aside with a gesture elephantine in strength but not quite disrespectful. The Brahmin tried elsewhere.

The pack of hounds was not trying elsewhere. It was still here, on their heels, keeping a safe distance, never losing contact, constantly changing its visible leaders, indefatigable. Colly decided there must be at least twenty of them: probably more. At least half could stop at any time and rest; could sleep for an hour or two until called forward again. He and Sandro could sit for a time, but not sleep, never sleep while the game went on, or the game would be over for good.

Meanwhile they were learning. He himself had a dozen faces clearly and permanently etched on the photographic plates of his mind, to join the faces that were already there. Sandro would have recorded the same faces and maybe others Colly had not spotted. More than this, Colly was now aware of professionalism, of training, of tight discipline and therefore of firm, experienced leadership.

This was not a collection of nuts, a maniac cult: these were professional criminals at least as adroit as all but the very best in Europe and America.

And the scale of the thing, the enormous, daunting size. This was a new lesson. They had known from the beginning that the thing was operating all over India. Dates and distances made it impossible that one group was responsible for all the disappearances, or two or three. They had assumed multiple little groups spread all across the subcontinent. Well, the groups were multiple all right, and they were spread across India, but they were not so little. Today proved that a big team of professionals could be whistled up and put in the field here in Benares. They could do that here; presumably they could do it in other places. In twenty other places? That made 400 people. In 100 other places? That made 2000 people. Add spies in police forces, hotels, maybe a lot of other useful sources of intelligence. That made an army.

It needed a whole national police effort to take on something this big: but the way things stood the police were checkmated before they started. All they had managed so far was to send a few plain-clothes men to almost certain death.

Colly and Sandro started moving again, as aimlessly as a saddhu and a holy sightseer might. They threaded the maze of little streets round the Golden Temple, and found the alley that led down to the Lalita Ghat on the riverbank. The alley was full of cows; a crowd of women was making, with busy slapping hands and interminable chatter, flat cakes out of the

fresh dung. The cakes were slapped on walls to dry;
then they would be fuel for cooking and for cremation.

The alley turned into a tunnel. It was dark. There
were no visible turnings off it. There were no people
in it: only a few of the sacred, pampered cows which
had wandered off in search of rubbish to nuzzle.

"Wrong turning," murmured Colly.

"Yes. But it is too late," said Sandro.

The pretence that they were not together had been
abandoned. In the eyes of the world there was still
no way they could be together; in the eyes of their
pursuers there was now no way they could be separate. Of course a spy in the hotel would already have
tied Sandro to Colly. They had not reckoned on
such a level of intelligence. They had not reckoned
on an enemy of such size and quality.

They had not reckoned on getting into a tunnel
without light or turnings or people.

"*Andiam,*" said Sandro.

"Yeah. Let's pick up our feet like rabbits."

They went on towards the river. For the benefit
of the women with the cows, still just visible, they
retained their respective manners of walking—Colly
his saddhu's trancelike strut, Sandro his priestly roll.
But they went faster.

In the bright patch of light behind them a group
appeared, advancing unhurriedly past the cows and
the women making dung-cakes. The pursuers would
look innocent enough to the women—simply an ill-
assorted collection of men brought by chance into a
kind of group, men of the most ordinary kinds, men
in no particular hurry, men sauntering, as hundreds
did, down towards the ghats reached by the tunnel.
But now they were a group. For their quarry they
had abandoned pretence. There was no longer need

of it. A dozen men filled the mouth of the tunnel, close together, coming towards them.

Sandro and Colly exchanged a glance. Sandro handed a cosh to Colly from the folds of his robe: flexible, heavily weighted, with a rawhide loop. Colly took it. He hefted it gently. It was a vicious and effective weapon, silent, difficult to see. It was reassuring to have it in his hand. He felt a moment's wry amusement: a near-naked, ash-daubed saddhu armed with a cosh was a wild contradiction. It no longer mattered. The situation was not really amusing.

They hurried towards the patch of light at the river end of the tunnel. It changed shape. Part was blackened by an irregular obstacle. Silhouetted against the glare from ghat and river, the obstacle was at first difficult to identify: then all too easy. It was another motley group of men, a dozen or more. The men were waiting in the mouth of the tunnel. At the distance, and in the conditions of light, there was nothing to identify the men, or show what they were waiting for. But there was no doubt who they were, or why they were there.

"Local knowledge," said Colly. "We could have used a little of that."

The group behind came steadily on.

It was quiet in the tunnel except for the distant chatter of the women, now out of sight, and the shifting feet and soft breathing of the sacred cows which had wandered away from the small herd in the alleyway.

They were indolent cows, torpid, overfed, their withers crowned with the high Brahman hump. They nuzzled at the rubbish in the tunnel. Flies covered them, and orbited noisily over their droppings. A homely, farmyard smell filled the tunnel from the droppings; the smell struck a bizarre note of the familiar, the comforting and domestic and healthy, in a situation of extreme danger.

The group in the riverward mouth of the tunnel advanced a little into the tunnel. The group was in no hurry. It came far enough into the tunnel, out of the brilliant sunlight which glared from the west across its mouth, to be out of sight of people on the ghat. The group numbered more than a dozen. No doubt they had left men at the mouth of the tunnel, to head off pilgrims who wanted to come away from the ghat. Those men would be reinforcements if needed; meanwhile they cut off all chance of help or of witnesses from the river.

The group behind continued unhurriedly down the tunnel towards the river. No doubt they also had left men stationed at the mouth nearest the city. These also would be reinforcements; they also cut off all hope of assistance.

There was no chance of two men, however armed, however skilled in man-to-man fighting, breaking through either group in the narrow space of the tunnel.

It was certain that, after these people had killed them, their bodies would disappear. This had happened in all cases. It was not clear how it had been managed in many of the cases of disappearance; it must sometimes have been difficult to arrange. In this case it would be easy. There were barges moored to the bank loaded with masonry for shoring up the bank against the tremendous flooding of the Ganges; their bodies would be weighted with chunks of masonry, and after dark they would go into the Ganges.

Sandro had a gun. He could use it to kill a few of these people. He proposed to do so. But rushed

from both sides he could hardly kill more than a
few. There were far more men coming at them than
there were rounds of ammunition in his automatic.
There would be no time to reload the magazine in
the handgrip from the box of shells in the waistband
under his robe.

Sandro had brought two knives also, spring-loaded
commando daggers, and the cosh which he had given
to Colly. Some damage could be done with these,
but not nearly enough. They could stand back to
back, but they would be overwhelmed. The men
would pour over them like the lava of Vesuvius en-
gulfing Pompeii.

Sandro stopped, and Colly with him. There was
no point in proceeding towards the group at the river
end, or of rushing back at the group at the landward
end. There was no point in stopping, either. It was
as easy to be killed in one place as in another.

A cow nuzzled at Sandro's robe, smelling in its un-
clean mustiness the possibility of pickings. It was a
cow of arrogant confidence, which from birth had
been treated with obsequious respect. It could get
away with anything. If it stole it committed no theft;
if it trampled a crop it honoured the man it bank-
rupted. It had none of the jitteriness of a cow in
any other country. It exercised a sacred right in brows-
ing at Sandro's robe.

Colly suddenly said, "Would you say these guys
are religious?"

"Come?"

"I was thinking about cows. I don't very often, but
just now I do."

He spoke casually, without haste or tremour. They
had faced death before. There was no hurry.

The group in front of them had again stopped, a

little way in from the mouth of the tunnel. The group behind advanced steadily, circumspectly. Nothing would happen for a minute or two.

"I don't mind committing a little sacrilege," said Colly. "But I wonder about old upper and nether millstones there."

"Good," said Sandro. "A little stampede."

"Which way?"

"To the river. Maybe we swim."

"Do you use the gun?"

"*Si, certo.* At the just moment. But first why not some heat? Why not a fire?"

"Why not? Plenty of garbage. Some dry, I guess, in spite of the cattle. We're in business. But not a fire in one spot, hey? Torches we can carry. Then we can go along with ol' Buttercup and her friends."

"*Giusto.*"

Under cover of the torpid cows they found enough dry paper—newspaper, the greasy wrappings of food —to make two good torches. Sandro had matches. Time was not yet short. It was a pity there were none of Shiva's buffaloes among the cows of Brahma.

Colly took one of Sandro's knives. He said, "Sorry, ma'am. I hate to do this."

He jabbed Sandro's cow in the rump with the point of the knife, to make sure it was thoroughly awake, angry, unnerved, before they lit the flares. The cow gave a squeal, of outraged dignity rather than of pain. It skittered on its narrow cloven feet across the ancient, greasy paving of the tunnel. It bumped into another cow, which grunted complainingly. Sandro jabbed the other cow. It squealed and broke into a sharp trot towards the river.

There were another ten cows scattered along the tunnel. Three were between the quarry and the landward pursuers, the rest between quarry and river.

Sandro lit his flare, and from it Colly's. They sputtered, smouldered, threatened to go out, then crackled and blazed. Sandro thrust the blazing bundle of paper at the tail of a cow on his landward side. The cow screamed and tried to bolt, but skidded for a moment helplessly on the greasy flagstones. Gritting his teeth, hating this, Sandro jabbed again at it with the torch. There was a sudden, sickening smell of singed hair and skin. The cow bellowed, and hurtled back along the tunnel. Its rage and panic infected the other two on its side; the three stampeded towards the group of pursuers.

He turned and joined Colly. With torches and knife-points they drove the cows towards the river. The cows went from nervous trot to hysterical gallop.

The cows rocketed down the tunnel. They squealed and bellowed; they cannoned into each other, and bounced off the walls of the tunnel. It was horribly possible that one or more would break a leg.

It occurred to Colly, even as he raced down the tunnel among the maddened cows, that he and Sandro could be in dire trouble with the Hindus, goading and stampeding the sacred cows in the holiest of Hindu cities. That was another problem for another day.

The cows were running in a loose bunch, like well-drilled rugby football forwards surging upfield. There were peewit cries of dismay from the men waiting near the mouth of the tunnel. The cows burst through the obstruction of the men as fermented liquor hurls the cork out of the neck of a bottle. A few of the men tried with shouts and waving to stop the cows. They were thrown aside or trampled by the sharp feet of the cows. Most of the men scattered in front of the cows, running for their lives out into the blazing afternoon sun.

The enemy in front was routed. For the moment.
The enemy behind? It was hard to see, with eyes
dazzled by the brief but intense glare of the paper
torches. Certainly the men behind had been ham-
pered by the three cows which had rushed at them.
But a dozen men bent on murder are not permanently defeated by three frightened cows. The delay
would be momentary.

They hurried towards the river in the wake of the
cows, which had now outdistanced them. Colly gave
Sandro back the cosh, which had been hanging by its
loop from his wrist, and the knife. He saw with regret that there was a little blood on the point of the
knife. Sandro hid the cosh and both knives under
his robes; he had already stowed away the gun. They
were all there if they were needed.

Just before they came out into the open, Colly and
Sandro resumed their characters and separateness.
Colly was ahead, blank-eyed, strutting unhurriedly;
Sandro rolled a few paces in his wake, his eyes bent
to the beads which he was telling with loud, irregular clicks. If both were dishevelled, it fitted the
character of both.

They passed a crowd of screeching women at the
edge of the Jalsain Ghat. There were older women
standing on ladders slapping cowdung cakes on to
the sunlit wall; at the foot of the ladders were girls
handing up the cowdung in fresh wet lumps. Close
by the women were big piles of wood. It was firewood. The cowdung was also for burning. The place
was a fuel store. This was a burning-ghat, a place of
Hindu cremation.

Turning a corner by the firewood, they came into
full view of the ghat. Behind, right up to the edge,
stood a tall jumble of temples. The ancient stones
of the ghat descended in steps to the mile-wide coffee-

coloured Ganges. Three funeral pyres were burning by the river. One had just been lit; the dry wood crackled furiously under the corpse, which was shrouded in a red sheet. On another the corpse was half consumed. There was not much left of a third corpse which lay on a bed of incandescent embers. Three other bodies were waiting to be burned, lying shrouded at the edge of the river, feet to the water, being sprinkled with holy drops from the Ganges. There were priests, parties of family mourners, and men with long sticks tending the fires.

Here and there stood the cows which had stampeded. Their eyes rolled and they were blowing and snuffing, but they had stopped running. They had evaded whatever threatened their rumps and their dignity; they had retained wariness but resumed arrogance.

Most of the men who had been in the mouth of the tunnel were on the ghat also. Some were in no shape to move, but at least a dozen were there, innocently standing or squatting, part of the scenery of the ghat, wholly unremarkable.

None of the priests or mourners seemed to be aware that anything unusual had happened. Yet they must have seen and heard the stampede of the cows, and the precipitate arrival of the men. Presumably priests and mourners had accepted that, on this day and at this hour, it was written that some sacred cows would pursue some men, with whatever damage was predestined to whichever of the men it was predestined for. They would assume that the men pursued by the cows, and those injured or killed, would accept the event with equal fatalism. What had happened, just as what would happen would happen. Meanwhile there were loved ones to be burned.

The attendant of the third fire heaved with his

stick the almost-consumed corpse off its bed of embers into the river. It hissed violently when it hit
the water, and stayed floating a foot from the bank.
Though most of it was burned, enough of it remained
to stick up hideously out of the water. Colly, reminded of barbecues, felt a little sick. The mourners
were unperturbed. They said some prayers and went
briskly away.

The rest of the pursuers came out of the tunnel,
and past the fuel store, and on to the ghat.

"Same situation as five hours ago," murmured Colly.
"Only now the cards are all on the table."

Eleven

Sandro and Colly squatted a little distance apart on the steps of the Jalsain Ghat. The sun was going down behind the ornate and spiky temples at their backs, turning the grey stone, badged here and there with gold, into a brooding purple.

The enormous yellowish river, darkening, was now almost empty of bathers. A few boats still dotted its surface. The far bank, to the south-east, was a limitless, featureless plain with no sign of humanity or habitation.

Cremation had almost finished for the day. The last two bodies were nearly consumed. Pungent smoke still rose from the embers.

Although a hundred teeming cities had poured their filth into the Ganges and Jumna, although hundreds of thousands of diseased people had bathed, although almost-burned corpses bobbed in the water like rubbish thrown from boats, the river looked quite clear and clean. Colly would not willingly have drunk it, but he could face swimming in it.

The cows had been respectfully herded away. A few mourners and priests remained; they would leave soon. The pursuers remained. They would not leave. They had drawn closer to Sandro and Colly. They formed a rough semicircle, squatting on the steps of the ghat, cutting their quarry off from all avenues of escape except the water. It was skilfully done. Leadership and discipline were again evident. The semicircle of watchers was regular enough to do its job: there were no gaps between men wide enough for a sudden burst to take the fugitives through. At the same time it was not so regular that it looked intentional.

"They can go faster on the land than we can go in the water," said Sandro.

"Yeah. Once we're in they can trot along the bank and stop us getting out. While they can see us. But once it gets properly dark . . ."

"They maybe have a boat with a big lamp, a searchlight."

"They maybe do. And with that many guys they can row it pretty quick. Suppose we swim clear across, starting now?"

"They get a boat. We do not reach the other side."

"Suppose . . ."

"*Ecco*," said Sandro.

Two boats had drifted downstream and now held their position, with easy occasional strokes of the oars, thirty yards from the steps of the ghat. There were four men in one of the boats and five in the other. No other boats in the river were stationary, except those moored or anchored; no others were near the Jalsain Ghat. There was no room for doubt about these two boats or about the men in them.

"I don't know just why," said Colly, "but I don't think those guys are drawn from the bunch we know and love. I think they're a new reserve, a new force they called up."

"*Si*, I think. As well as an army they have a navy."

"Next thing you know the sky will be full of goddam helicopters . . . . Pretty soon it's gonna be dark."

"Yes. That makes it possible for us, maybe."

"And possible for them."

"That also."

"That barge," said Colly. "The one full of rocks."

"Yes?"

"Tied up one end, anchored the other."

"Yes. We can get aboard on those ropes."

"But without the ropes the freeboard's too high for anybody to climb up out of the water."

"They climb from their boats."

"We sink their boats."

"With the large rocks in the barge. Good. We sink some of them too, maybe."

"There's two tricks here, chum, and both look a little tricky from where I sit. We have to get into the water, out to the barge, up those ropes, before they know what we're doing. And we have to cast off or cut free before they can follow us up."

"Yes. I think we fail. But it is better to try something."

"Just for laughs. Just not to get bored, hunkering here."

They waited a little longer, while the sun went fully down behind the towers and temples of the city. It was still very hot. The sky grew rapidly darker; over the great flatland to the south east it shaded from purple to black. The river was a mile of ink.

The last of the funeral pyres sank to dark embers. The last of the priests and mourners hurried away.

The ring of the pursuers began to close in. The two boats in the river edged nearer to the steps of the ghat.

"About now?" asked Colly.

"*Si. Andiam.*"

When they moved they moved fast.

They jumped to their feet, side by side on the edge of the river. Sandro shrugged off the huge horse-

blanket in which he was shrouded, and threw aside
the tall Tam-o'-Shanter on his head. They projected
themselves in simultaneous flat dives from the ghat
into the black water. Sandro swam to the long rope
which moored the barge to a rotting hulk by the
riverbank; Colly swam to the barge's anchor-rope.
Each grabbed his rope and went up it hand over
hand.

A series of splashes at the edge of the water showed
that most of the pursuers on the ghat had gone into
the water after them. There were shouts from the
ghat, answered from the two boats. The shouts were
not in a language Sandro had ever heard.

One of the pursuers was a fine swimmer. He reached
the mooring-rope when Sandro was still halfway up
it. He began to swarm up the rope with the agility
of a spider. It was very brave of him to follow, on
his own, a man of Sandro's size. It was very foolish.
Sandro waited for a second, then jackknifed at the
waist and kicked out, catching the man full in the
face with both heels. Sandro had lost his sandals in
the water but his bare heels were hard enough to
kill. The man's head jerked back and he fell without
a sound off the rope into the water.

Colly was already aboard, dripping and almost
naked, the ash washed from his body, his wild hair
and beard draggled and streaming with Ganges water. He was heaving at the anchor-rope so that he
could free it. A swimmer reached the anchor-rope
and began to climb it. There were three more swimmers close behind him. Colly picked up a piece of
rock the size of a football and hurled it at the man
on the rope. There was a crunch as it hit him on
the shoulder. The man screamed and fell into the
water. Immediately another started up the rope.

At the same moment one of the rowing boats

bumped against the side of the barge. Sandro prized a rock the size of an armchair, insecure near the gunwale of the barge, free of the pile of rocks. He tried to roll it over the gunwale, exerting every ounce of his enormous strength. His muscles screamed with the effort and the roughness of the rock lacerated his hands. Men were standing up in the boat, reaching for the gunwale. In a second three or more would be up. With a final heave, and a roar of supreme physical effort, Sandro rolled the rock over the gunwale. It crashed through the bottom of the rowing boat; the rowing boat had no bottom; it was broken in half and awash. The rock hit the legs of the man rowing the boat. It smashed them too. One of the men from the boat was half over the gunwale of the barge. He was reaching out at Sandro. As Sandro straightened to hit him he was grabbed from behind.

The other rowing boat had crept up to the barge on the other side. The men were aboard the barge. Two more men were climbing the anchor-rope.

Sandro kicked out at the man on the barge's gunwale. He brought the heel of his hand down on the side of the neck of the man who had grabbed him. The man was strong and wiry but not very heavy. He went down hard on the rocks in the barge. It occurred to Sandro, with relief and great surprise, that these men had no knives. He bellowed. He knocked a man off the barge into the water with his fist. He was grabbed again; he shook off his attacker and hit him in the solar plexus.

Colly had hit another man with a rock and knocked him off the anchor-rope. He could guard the rope without trouble. But some of the swimmers had climbed into the second rowing-boat and were swarming from it on to the barge. Colly could find no more rocks small enough to throw. He and Sandro rushed together at the new wave of boarders. There were five of the pursuers now aboard the barge. They were stronger than they looked and fought with skill and ferocity. More men were coming up both the mooring-rope and the anchor-rope.

Sandro's gun was useless and he had lost one of his knives during the swim or the fight. With a great heave he freed one arm from the grip of two men and pulled his remaining knife from his waistband. The blade clicked out on the spring. He jabbed indiscriminately at dark wet heads and hands and shoulders. There were screams and sobs.

Colly ran to the anchor-rope. He knocked out a man who was just coming over the gunwale. Heaving, he managed to slip the loop at the end of the rope clear of the kind of rough cleat which held it. He dropped the rope into the water.

The barge began to swing with the current. It was still moored to the hulk by its other end.

Colly hurried to help Sandro. In the near darkness it was difficult to hurry across the uneven mass of rocks in the barge. He fell heavily, gashing himself on a sharp edge of rock. He grabbed a brown ankle and heaved. The leg kicked out at his head, quick and skilful. He just avoided the full force of the kick; he kept hold of the ankle and twisted it sharply. The man let go of Sandro's waist and crashed onto the rocks. He was knocked out.

Sandro only had three or four men to cope with. He could manage for a little while with these odds, because of his gigantic strength and because he had a sharp and heavy knife.

Colly hurried to the mooring-rope. He tried to cast off. There was a huge, amateurish knot securing the rope to a great iron ring on the gunwale of the barge. It was impossible to see to undo the knot. Sandro was using, and needed, their only knife. There were men in the water near the rope but none was yet climbing the rope.

Colly ran back to Sandro. Chopping, punching, gouging, he bundled two of them overboard. Sandro hit a third so hard that he rose in the air before crashing down on to the rocks. They threw a fourth overboard between them. The boat was still below, with two men in it. Other men were swimming towards it and there must now be men on the mooring-rope. Sandro began to heave a rock over the gunwale. With Colly's help it was easier this time. The rock was poised for a second on the gunwale. The men in the boat saw the threat. They pushed the boat away from the barge just as the rock fell. The rock caught the point of the bows of the boat, shattering the wood and the head of the man who was crouched in the bows.

A man was coming over the gunwale by the mooring-rope. Another was close behind him. These people were very brave, especially as they all fought without knives. Sandro and Colly knocked both men back into the water. Sandro grunted with dismay when he saw the size of the mooring-rope; it would take a long time to cut. More reinforcements might by then have been called up, more boats, knives, ropes, maybe guns.

Sandro guessed that the wood of the barge might, just might, be a little rotten. He took hold of the iron ring bolted to the gunwale and heaved. There was a noise of splintering; wood powdered away; the huge rusty bolts jumped clear of the wood. Sandro tossed the iron ring, and with it the mooring-rope, into the black water.

The barge was adrift. They were safe.

"What do we do with the supercargo?" asked Colly. "Pitch them overboard?"

Sandro grunted dubiously. It was obviously sensible, but it was repugnant to pitch unconscious or disabled men into an enormous river.

"They will not answer any questions, from us or from anybody."

"Nope. They're religious fanatics. And goddam brave with it."

"Then we leave them in command. They are prize-crew."

"They are tigers, creatures of the jungle."

"Yes. We will kill them as man-eating tigers are killed, with stealth and great preparation and overwhelming strength."

The train chugged slowly across the desert, due westwards from Delhi. Dawn was cool and pink: mid-morning was white hot. The desert was an infinity of buff-coloured dust. Yet there were people in it. Veena saw from the windows of the tinny, biscuit-box carriage villages dotting the desert like clumps of dusty mole-hills. Round the villages there were people in surprising numbers, visible from a great distance because of the brightness of their clothes—brilliant saris, tall red turbans, the glint of profuse golden ornament. The people herded goats, squatting in the narrow shade of desiccated trees, or scratched at the dusty ground with mattocks. Veena was amazed that the harsh landscape could support any life at all. It seemed to her that she was used to green, to fat grass and big trees, to copious water.

But Kashi said that this was her homeland: Kashi her protector, her future husband, Kashi who said that he loved her. It must be true. Veena believed him completely.

During the hot, weary hours of the journey Kashi explained to her about herself, since she had lost her memory because of her illness.

She understood why her homeland was strange to her, and why she spoke and thought in English when she was a dark-skinned and jet-haired Indian.

Her parents had gone to England, when newly married, as the servants of a Sahib's family. She had been born there, brought up entirely there, taught to speak only English, accustomed only to English food and manners. After the early death of both her parents she had been virtually adopted by the Sahib, the English colonel. It was kind of him but it was wrong. She had seen that it was wrong. She had returned to India seeking, so she had said before her illness, her own roots. She had studied Hindi and Hinduism. She had met Kashi, himself a widower, a cattle-owning member of her own caste. She had, alas, no family and therefore no dowry, but she had inherited from her mother the few golden ornaments that she now wore. Kashi was not concerned with dowry on account of his great love for her.

"Why do you have another name?" asked Veena. "What does it mean?"

"Feringhia. It conveys Frankish, foreign, European, you know? It was the name given to a quite distinguished ancestor of mine, because Europeans were involved in some quite violent way at the time of his birth. So his mother chose the name. He went on to become famous, a leader of his own people and pretty well known to the English, too. By chance the same kind of thing happened at the time of my own birth. That was in 1929, and India was in a turmoil sometimes, revolutionaries, the struggle for independence. My own family was *not* involved in all that. Country people were not involved at all, it was all in the big towns. But there were soldiers and police and arrests, so I was called Feringhia as a kind of nickname, and in memory of my distinguished ancestor. Only my old friends and my family use the name. Kashi is my real name, you know. Kashi Nath Rao."

"You speak English very well, Kashi."

"Oh yes. We speak it at home quite a lot. Also a mixture of Hindi, Hindustani, Rajasthani and Ramasi."

"Ramasi?"

"That is another language you will be learning, dear Veena. Your children must be brought up to speak Ramasi."

Veena nodded submissively.

They got off the train in a rambling, dusty town that smelled of desperate poverty. Kashi helped Veena into a horse-drawn tonga. The horse could hardly pull their combined weight and that of the driver. It was terribly thin, with a toast-rack chest, cut and bruised legs with swollen knees, and sores all over its miserable back. The driver whacked at it continually with a stick.

"Poor horse," said Veena to Kashi.

"Yes. But it is the only way to get home. You are remembering English horses, the horses of the English colonel?"

"Am I?"

"It is different here. This man has to feed his family, and then there is nothing left for the horse."

The streets of the town were narrow and serpentine. Many were lined by open drains, slimy and stinking. There were stray dogs everywhere, which had scratched themselves hairless.

"Poor dogs," said Veena.

Kashi smiled but said nothing.

She supposed this was another bit of Englishness, learned from life with the Colonel Sahib, which she must now forget.

The tonga jingled clear of the town, its horse tottering, ceaselessly beaten, looking on the point of death. They crossed miles of arid flatlands with a few outcrops of yellow-grey stone and a very few stunted trees. They were a long time on this stage of the journey; the distance was not great but the horse moved slowly. Their speed was not enough to be cool. It was terribly hot. The sun hit like a policeman's iron-bound lathi, and glared off the stony vastness of the land. Veena's eyes smarted and her head swam.

They came at last to the village. It was small—a huddle of little flat-roofed houses, mostly of one room only, most of mud, a few white-washed. Women in brilliant-coloured saris squatted at every door, cooking or plaiting their hair or chattering loudly to neighbours. Everywhere there were children and goats. A few small trees grew at the edge of the village, in which vultures and kites roosted like enormous fruit.

The arrival of the tonga caused immediate and intense excitement. Veena realised that Kashi was expected, and that he was a man of great note here. It occurred to her that she also was expected. The village had heard of Kashi's bride. The people were agog to see her. Women in astonishing numbers poured out of the tiny houses, pulling their veils over their faces; men hurried up, shouting, from the tiny bazaar or the cattle-pens or the nearest fields. Children swarmed towards the tonga, screeching and pointing, or clung to their mothers' saris. Dogs barked; goats stampeded; a few vultures flopped along the stony ground. There was a deafening noise, all of welcome, all of the greatest good-nature.

Kashi directed the tonga-wallah to a whitewashed mud house, a very little larger than the rest; it stood at the edge of the village, with a walled yard behind full of cows and buffaloes. The whole crowd followed, still shouting joyously, and surrounded the tonga when it stopped. The bravest children reached up to touch Veena's arm, shrieking at their own audacity.

A woman of about sixty hurried out of the house, wiping her hands on the hem of her sari; her plump golden face was cut into two by the breadth and excitement of her smile. She wore a heavy gold ring in her nostril, and her neck, ears and arms were loaded with golden ornaments of heavy local workmanship. Like everyone else she was barefooted. She pulled Veena into the house and sat her on a string hammock; she patted her arm incessantly, loving and welcoming, too excited to speak. The floor of the house was trodden earth, the walls whitewashed inside as well as out. Steep stairs led to the roof. Gaudy pictures of gods were stuck to the walls. Most were highly coloured and sentimental, smiling pink-and-white godlings with cupid's-bow mouths. One was in the sharpest contrast; Veena recognized Kali, black, capering, hideous.

Kashi presented Veena to his mother. Veena was happily aware, at once, of a real and affectionate welcome. The old lady spoke fair English; she said she understood that Veena was strange to the ways of her own people, that everyone understood, that everyone would help, that Kashi's chosen bride brought the greatest happiness to her house.

Tired and confused, Veena felt tears prick her eyes at the unaffected warmth of this greeting.

Women and children jostled at the door of the little house. Kashi, laughing, made some kind of speech to them, introduced his bride to his neighbours. It was greeted with almost hysterical joy and applause. The more important ladies of the village were introduced one by one; to each, instructed by Kashi, Veena bowed with hands joined.

The wedding was to be almost at once.

Twelve

Travellers continued to disappear, all over India, at, perhaps, a slightly faster rate. Still no women were taken—no other women. Still no bodies were found. Still no witnesses came forward with anything helpful to the police. Still police spies, wherever posted, came back empty handed: or failed to come back.

Colly's account of the murders he had seen was on file. No one believed a word of it.

Colly and Sandro visited a number of places in the Plain of the Ganges where disappearances had occurred. Sometimes they were in disguise, sometimes not. Usually they adopted a kind of disguise meant to be penetrated. They were followed and watched all the time. It was well done, but not quite well enough for them to be unaware of it. They tried several times to ambush a watcher. The only time they succeeded the man had a fit. A doctor said it was epilepsy and the man was near death.

They were not attacked or harassed in any way: simply watched.

They were driven three-quarters mad by their helplessness. Still no ransom demand came; nothing came; with each hour that went by the chance of a message was smaller. Why should a kidnapper wait?

They had learned something in the back alleys of

Benares, and on the burning-ghat, and on the stone-barge. They had learned that they could not take on this thing without an army: but also that no useful army could be recruited locally, because of security leaks, and none could be brought in from outside.

Veena fell easily into the routine of the village and of the house of Muni, her future mother-in-law.

As soon as the cool pink sun lifted over the rim of the desert there came, from all around, the clash of brass pots and jugs. Veena would at once join the other women among the houses, and walk with them, all chattering like birds, to the well which was the preserve of their caste. She learned quickly, since her figure was upright and her carriage graceful, to balance a great brass bowl on a pad on her head.

Then she helped feed chaff from a bunker to the cattle in the pen, and to carry the fresh milk as it was drawn from the cows and buffaloes. Immediately she helped Muni to rake the night's dung into a pile, knead it with bare feet into a proper texture, shape it into cakes by hand, and slap the cakes in rows on to a wall to dry. It was necessary then to bathe with ritual thoroughness before eating, although cow-dung, the emission of a sacred animal, is not in the least dirty.

Veena helped Muni make wheaten chappatis and savoury vegetable curries, and yoghurt and curds and cheese. She carried milk to the bazaar for sale. Becoming daily more fluent, speaking no English, she chattered to the other women of the village and played with the swarms of children.

In the cool of the evening the household, like every other, climbed up to the roof after dinner; they sat by oil-lamp or moonlight, with the huge desert stretching all round, its savagery muted by darkness. Sometimes Muni sang, or the children of the aunts and cousins who made up the household. (There were many men besides Kashi, but all were away on unexplained business. He received frequent messages from them; he seemed to Veena to be in some sort in charge of these male relations, although not with them because of his forthcoming marriage.)

They all slept on the roof. The sky was cool and full of stars.

Veena began to learn Ramasi, a language known to, but not usually used by, everyone in the village: a language with no relationship to any other that Veena had met.

She did not understand why the villagers all knew a language additional to all the ordinary languages of India. She realised that it was special to certain people, of whom she was now, or would shortly be, one. She did understand that this was why she herself must learn it, and why her children must learn it. She did not know what was special about herself, her new family, the neighbours. She accepted it placidly, as something which was written. She had acquired, as though born to it, the docility of Indian women and the fatalism of all Indians. She accepted that she would marry Kashi and that her children would be Kashi's.

It did not seem to her that she had chosen Kashi—that he had sought her acceptance of her hand and been granted it. It seemed to her that she was obliged, by forces entirely beyond her control or understanding, to marry him. It was what she was to do: there was an end of it.

She accepted this fate without excitement but without repugnance. Kashi was as considerate and gentle as a man could be. He was evidently a very good son to Muni, a popular and respected man in the village, absolutely honest in his dealings, trusted, often consulted. He was generous with alms and with help to his friends. He was intelligent and interesting. Though not widely read, he had travelled a great deal in every part of India except the south, and told Veena much that interested and amused her.

Veena's future was clear. It was in no doubt. Everybody in the village knew it. She was fully adjusted to the prospect. In any case she had no choice. Had Kashi been odious to her, the village hateful, she could not have left. She was never alone. Dozens of people were always about her, every one of whom knew her, every one of whom was loyal to Kashi. She could not, by day or night, have crossed the desert to the nearest town.

The wedding was imminent, the date having been established by reference to horoscopes.

Three weeks had crawled by. To wait was no longer endurable.

Ishur Ghose seemed to have suffered as much as Sandro and Colly. He blamed himself, though they told him not to: he had aged, shrunk; the affable torrent of his conversation slowed to an unhappy dribble.

Colly said, "That's it. No message. No hope."

"No," said Sandro.

"Let's go out and hit them."

"How?" asked Ishur Ghose.

"We'll find some. We did before, we can again. Or they'll find us. They know what we look like. We'll meet them, a bunch of them, and—"

"Use guns," said Sandro.

"Yes, guns."

"You will be killed," said Ishur Ghose.

Colly looked at him woodenly. "Do you think we care?"

Sandro said, "We will maybe not be killed, not at once. If we are killed it will not be before we have done much killing. The people who attacked us in Benares were not armed. Or, if they had guns or knives, they did not use them. We shall kill many of them, *molti molti.*"

"Is that right? Right to do? Morally right?" asked the gentle old Indian.

"Yes," said Colly. "They killed nearly a thousand people, and one of them is Jenny, and nobody even dented them yet."

Muni talked long to Veena, in the soft cool evenings on the roof of the white house.

From the old woman Veena learned that many things had enabled the people—the people who were now her people—to survive and flourish from their birth at the very dawn of the world. Veena learned about their absolute secrecy, their private language of signals and speech, their knowledge of what was to be done by others, which came from the highest government offices and flew from one end of India to the other. She knew that the people—like other peoples—inherited strictly from father to son, and no son could escape his destiny; that they had now, as they had always had, a blinding religious certainty about the sanctity of their form of worshipping the Goddess Kali.

And this also had protected them, Veena learned: when not on expedition, they were respectable citizens, hard-working farmers, officials of unusual honesty, or diligent craftsmen. They were law-abiding, thrifty, and of good report.

"Like Kashi," said Veena.

"Like Kashi, and like his friends. Your friends."

No breath of suspicion attached to any of them, anywhere in India. They were often leading members of the communities in which they lived, exceptional only in their extended absences from home.

Sometimes not even in this: for there had been, said Muni, many whole villages in which every household had been born into the brotherhood. Now there were again such villages. One was the home of Muni and Kashi and now of Veena.

Veena saw that some of the older men, older even than Sanghavi, left the village on expeditions. This surprised her, as she was beginning to understand that their worship of Kali required a man to be strong and active and quick in his movements.

Muni explained that when men grew too old for the rigours of the expeditions, their devotion and their usefulness were by no means at an end. They became watchmen, spies, or dressers of food.

"Very many of us," said Muni, "have become important men in the councils of princes. Some have been tax-collectors. Some now are officers in the police. When these ones become old, they can still tell us very many things which it is useful for us to know."

Veena nodded, dutifully learning.

Muni said, "The same is true of us, of wives and female relatives. We are usually of the same inheritance as our men. You are an exception, dear Veena, because my son saw and loved you, and knew you would be a good mother to his sons. We understand, though we do not share, the work and worship of our menfolk."

"It is an honour," said Veena.

"Yes. It is an honour."

"Now?" said Colly.

"Now," said Sandro.

"Very well," sighed Ishur Ghose. "Tell me if I can be of any help."

The old man hobbled out to visit a friend, but said that he would be back; he begged them not to set off on their battle until he had seen them again.

"I thought," said Veena, one evening of particular beauty, when soft music came from the neighbouring rooftops, and the cattle stamped and breathed contentedly in their pen, "I thought our people were destroyed by the English."

"The English thought otherwise," said Muni. She laughed gently. "They condemned our women to solitary lives so that they should breed no more of our people. But some whom they so condemned were already great with child. The children were born into our brotherhood and the heritage of the brotherhood. But our people were asleep for a long time. We waited, hiding, biding our time, endlessly patient. We never forgot who we were, but our ancestors sinned, and the judgement of Kali was that we should spend long years waiting for her sign. Then came a man who had the sign. He showed it to us. He was an old man, much older even than I. He was a great scholar. He had been important and trusted in the government, so that he knew many secrets. He is still trusted in the government, and he still knows many secrets. It is of great help and value. He was the midwife of our rebirth."

"May he help us for a long time," said Veena.

"That is our prayer."

Ishur Ghose's telephone rang. Colly answered it. The voice was strange: a young man, speaking good but flowery English. He said the young lady from foreign-side was alive. She was quite well, in satisfactory health. She was a prisoner but well treated. Where she was neither they nor anyone could find her. He could vouch for that, give a one hundred percent guarantee. But she would soon be near Bombay. Not tomorrow or the next day, but in eight days or perhaps ten or twelve or twenty. Not in Bombay but fifty miles away. She would be at Ajanta or Ellora, the great temples. There was a reason for her to be taken there. The caller knew this beyond possibility of doubt. He was telling them, at great risk to himself, because he did not approve of the abduction of women, of young female persons. It was a dreadful way to behave, and disgrace to the new India. He was calling from nearby, from Ramnagar. His name was of no importance. He wanted neither rewards nor even thanks.

Ishur Ghose, late at night, read one of his old books, sent to him from Calcutta. He was smoking his English pipe.

He read an English translation of the account, written in 1666, by the French traveller Thevenot, of the many mysterious deaths on the roads of India, and of the sect responsible for them:

"They have another cunning trick, also, to catch travellers with. They send out a handsome woman upon the road who, with her hair dishevelled, seems to be all in tears, sighing and complaining of some misfortune which she pretends has befallen her. Now, as she takes the same way as the traveller goes, he easily falls into conversation with her and, finding her beautiful, offers her his assistance, which she accepts. But he hath no sooner taken her up behind him on horseback, but she throws the snare about his neck and strangles him; or at least stuns him, until the

robbers—who lie hid—come running to her assistance
and complete what she hath begun."

"I make a journey," said Kashi to Veena in Hindi.
"Yes?"

"This time you will come with me."

"Very well," said Veena, pleased. "A journey to
what place?"

"A long way, to a very great and ancient temple,
a wonder of the world, a most sacred place to us."

"Very well."

"There is a thing that must be done. Then we
shall come back for the wedding."

They smiled at each other under the stars; Muni
gurgled sentimentally.

It was an important expedition. The pujah that
preceded it was of exceptional length and complexity.

Veena did not see or hear the ceremony, nor would
she ever do so, but she was aware that it was being
held.

She knew—Muni had taught her—that departure
might not be announced on any Wednesday or Thurs-
day, or in any day in July, September or December.

She knew that after departure was announced, it
was necessary to wait for the omens. There were very
many omens, favourable and unfavourable, which
were the secret messages of the Goddess Kali to her
secret followers, and understood only by them.

After days of waiting, Kashi came home in unusual
excitement. He reported that the cry of a crane had
been heard on the left hand followed by the cry of
a crane on the right hand. This was an excellent
omen for departure.

The men who were coming with them on their
journey fasted for seven days, eating only fish, dal,

which was dried beans, and gur, which was unrefined sugar, and of special magical importance. The men did not shave their faces, nor wash their garments, nor give alms during the seven days. All feasted on green vegetables on the seventh day.

After an expedition had started, Kashi told Veena, stricter men did not brush their teeth unless the expedition lasted for more than a year. Smiling, he said that although they were careful to keep all their ancient laws, this one few of them kept.

Thirteen

Veena's curry was in a special dish. She looked questioningly at Muni. Muni smiled with her usual placid affection.

Kashi said, "It is a special dish because you are a special person."

Veena did not want to be a special person, but she ate her curry obediently from the earthenware bowl that Muni gave her. It was stronger than usual, very hot and pungent. She liked it. It looked and smelled like the curry the others were eating. She did not know what was special about it, but there was much she did not yet understand.

Veena slept more deeply than usual the night after eating the special curry. She began to yawn, helplessly, hugely, even before the family went up the narrow stairs to the roof.

Muni looked at her lovingly, with a Cheshire-cat smile that outshone the lamps in the house and the bright pictures of gods on the whitewashed walls; the smile was all that Veena could see, and the last thing she saw until she awoke, gummy-eyed and heavy-limbed, in the pearly morning.

She did not attach any meaning to the once-beautiful, deeply-stained piece of green silk hung out to dry on the low wall at the edge of the roof.

* * *

The journey to Bombay was complicated and slow. It involved many changes of train, many long waits at stations all down the west-centre of India. Veena found it tiring but quite interesting. Kashi was endlessly kind, concerned always to see that she was comfortable, that she had what she wanted to eat and drink, that she was kept amused. Five men came with them from the village. It seemed they were to meet others at the great temple. It was a sort of pilgrimage. There were holy things that Veena must see before she married Kashi.

Their five companions were as gentle and considerate as Kashi himself. Veena knew them all, but slightly; they had been away from the village most of the time that she had been there. They treated Kashi with a mixture of respect and old friendship. He was the chief of them, very evidently the chief of them, but they felt for him a visible warm affection as well as a disciplined respect. They called him 'Jemadar' or 'Feringhia' when there were no strangers by, but called him 'Kashi' in public.

They stopped for the second night at a small station in the foothills of the Satpuras. The gentle, ageing man called Sanghavi stayed with Veena. He looked after her. She knew she was perfectly safe with him, and she was; she settled herself to sleep on rugs on the platform of the station. Kashi and the others went away. They said they had a religious duty to perform. Veena accepted this without surprise. She knew that Kashi was deeply religious; she knew that she, and even Muni, and the other women of their village, were debarred from some of the rites and acts of worship which were important to Kashi and his friends.

Strolling near the station in the cool of the early evening, Kashi and the other men had been visibly

alerted by things which Veena herself had not par-
ticularly noticed, the cawing of crows, the braying of
donkeys, some birds in the sky. Veena did not know
why these omens were suddenly important. But there
was much she did not understand. Her faith in Kashi
was absolute. She settled herself to sleep, unworried,
on the rugs Sanghavi spread for her on the station
platform.

The two Bhil farmers were tired. They had walked
all day and they still had a long way to walk. But
if the lawsuit were decided in their absence, paid witnesses would swear to so many lies that their case
would be lost and judgement against them would
be ruin.

They were glad to meet the party of Rajasthanis,
farmers like themselves.

They squatted by small cooking-fires by the dusty
side-road, the Bhils and their new friends. They were
on a strip of ground, much used as a camping place
on account of a water-tank, between the road and
freshly-ploughed field. It was very dark away from
the fires. When the fires burned low the men could
barely see each other. The Bhils stretched themselves
out to sleep; they had come a long way and they
had a long way to go. They lay so that under their
bodies were the pouches of money hidden in their
dhotis. They had collected all possible funds so that
they could meet the bought evidence of their enemies
with well-rehearsed witnesses of their own. They did
not mention the money. They trusted the Rajasthanis, who were poor men oppressed like themselves,
but they did not trust them so far as to mention the
money. It had been borrowed at a high rate of interest from a money-lender in Barwani.

One of the Bhils slept. The other mumbled, sighed,
yawned, shifted his position.

Feringhia said, "Give me a bidi, Lal Chand."

As he gave this understood signal, he drew from his shirt a scarf of yellow and white cotton, narrow and knotted, with a slip-knot. One of his companions drew out a similar scarf. At the same moment the other two men fell on the Bhils. Normally two men would have fallen upon each victim, but one Bhil was asleep and the other nearly so, and the Jemadar had decided that one limb-holder would do for each. The Bhils were little men, not young. The limb-holders, with the skill of long practice, secured the arms and legs of the Bhils, who hardly had time to wake and struggle before they felt the Ruhmal tightening round their necks.

Feringhia and the other strangler killed the two Bhils quite quickly. There was no further sound. There was no mark on the bodies except that of the cotton scarves which had strangled them.

Carefully, decently, without haste or hesitation, Feringhia and his companions stripped the bodies. They found the pouches of money. They placed them by one of the almost-dead cooking fires. Feringhia took out a knife which he used for no other purpose; he opened up the bodies so that they would not swell from gassification after burial in the hot ground. He disjointed the bodies and folded them into compact parcels.

The fifth man of the party had up until now squatted a few paces away. He watched with serious professional interest, just able to see in the darkness actions he had seen so very many times. Now his own duty was to be performed. He drew from his waistband the head of a small pickaxe, and into it fitted a piece of wood which he had been using as a staff. He dug a single grave for the two men, digging quickly and expertly in the soft ground at the edge of the ploughed field. He covered the bodies, and with the blade of his pickaxe reshaped the earth exactly as it had been left by the plough. The bodies were deep enough so that no plough or mattock would uncover them. There was earth left over, a pile of earth neatly mounded on the garment of one of the Bhils, for which there had been no room in the grave, since the little folded bodies now occupied the space which this earth had occupied. The digger of graves broadcast the extra earth far and wide over the field. It drifted over the broken ground like powder.

Feringhia spread a rug on the ground. He and the other strangler sat on the rug, facing westwards; the three others squatted behind them. Kussi, the head of the pickaxe, lay in front of them with a coin from one of the pouches, a silver coin intended for bribing witnesses in the lawcourts but now more honourably used to the glory of Kali.

Feringhia prayed. His companions echoed his prayers, softly, solemnly.

Feringhia took a little unrefined sugar from a hollow in the ground in front of him, placing some on the palm of the other strangler and some on his own palm. He and the other ate the sacred gur.

The grave-digger buried his pickaxe in a few inches of earth at the edge of the ploughed field. The blade pointed towards Bombay.

All sighed, smiled to each other in the darkness, and settled down to sleep. Feringhia's head, on a pillow which had been the dhoti of a Bhil, lay within a yard of the new grave. He would have slept, for choice, directly on the grave, but he did not wish to lie on ploughed ground.

They slept peacefully.

When the sky first began to lighten Feringhia awoke. He woke those of his companions who were still asleep. The gravedigger dug up the pickaxe. It had not moved in the night; the goddess approved the direction of their journey.

They examined the grave, and made finishing touches to the earth above it. The ground looked completely undisturbed. Feringhia looked critically round their camping-place. The cooking-fires were cold, and were two among fifty scarred black circles on this patch of ground beside the road. Paper and cigarette-ends that they had dropped were lost in drifts of waste paper and wide-strewn butts of cheap cigarettes.

They still had the world to themselves, a milky dawn not yet full of the clang of waterpots at the well-head or the lowing of cattle being fed.

Veena awoke, stiff but refreshed by a tranquil sleep on the station platform. Kashi was there. He and the others had returned from their religious duties. Veena was glad. She smiled at Kashi. He said that the gods had been kind. He and the others were in high spirits.

"I understand, Jemadar, that the two must be killed," said Lal Chand. "But I do not understand why we must cross India to kill them."

Feringhia said, "Our people have never killed a Frank, neither recently nor in the old days. It is not clear to us how Bhowani will like such a sacrifice. For this reason it is ordered that the two shall be killed in a place very holy to Bhowani and to us. It might have been at Kalighat or at Bindachun, but a shikar in those places would be very difficult."

"That is so. Very many worshippers, and a lot of fat priests with bright eyes."

"We choose therefore an equally holy place where

there will be no difficulty. The one equally holy place where there will be no crowds of worshippers, and we can hide what we do from the bright eyes of the fat priests."

"Ellora. Of course."

"Of course. And I am encouraged to believe that Bhowani approves of the plan."

"It is evident that She does, since She sent us those two little Bhils with more money than could have been believed possible. At the same time, Jemadar, there will be a certain difficulty. The two will be alert and suspicious, on their guard, after the events at the Pilgrim House, and the events on the barge at Varanasi, and after the message which they have received on the telephone."

"That is true, and it is part of the reason why Veena accompanies us."

"Does she know that she is to be a decoy?"

"Does the tethered goat know that it decoys the tiger?"

"The goat is killed."

"What will be will be, but these tigers will not wish to kill this goat."

"They will wish to kill the shikaris."

"Yes, but the shikaris will be safe in the hide."

"While the goat is tethered as it were to a tree . . . There is in truth no need for Veena to be there at all, Jemadar. Our tigers will come, hoping to find her, whether she is there or not."

"Of course, but she accompanies us nonetheless, and for two reasons. The small and unimportant reason is that, although we will be many and they but two, they will *not* be easy to kill. Even if we have Veena with us it will not be easy: but if we do not have Veena it will be less easy still."

"I do not think that is an altogether small and

unimportant reason, Jemadar. What is the larger reason?"

"Veena should herself make pilgrimage to Ellora. Saving only those two others, it is the place in all the world most sacred to the Goddess. My bride should make herself known to the Goddess at one of Her most favoured shrines."

"Is this the counsel of the midwife of our rebirth?"

"Surely. All that now goes forward is strictly as he himself advised. Everything is thought of, Lal Chand, and the plan is made."

"It's a trap," said Colly.

"*Si*. There is no choice but to walk into it."

"I respectfully concur," said Ishur Ghose.

The old man was filling his pipe, ritualistically going through the motions he had learned long before from the Sahibs.

He said, from a cloud of smoke, "I am terribly tempted to come with you. It is donkey's years since I saw those places. Of course the religious aspect is awful rubbish, pure idolatry actually, but there is quite a lot to interest a bloke with my ethnological tastes."

"Do these temples have any link to Kalighat or Bindachun?"

"Oh, hardly. Ajanta is entirely Buddhist, you know. Buddhism was all the rage in India for a few centuries. Then we relapsed back into Hinduism, which perhaps suits better the funny old Indian character. Some of Ellora is Buddhist, but the main part is Hindu. Kali is there, I expect, since the great temple is Shiva's. I don't remember what form she takes. It's not a place where dreadful blokes go to cut off the heads of animals. They don't have any of that distasteful mumbo-jumbo. So you'll go there in a few

days to rescue your fair maiden? You're biting off
the devil of a lot, if you'll forgive my pointing it
out. What about a few policemen to help you?"

"No," said Sandro at once. "If we arrive with policemen we will never see any of them. And we will
never see Jenny, even if she is there."

"Policemen in reserve?" suggested Ishur Ghose. "If
you get a message to me . . ."

"Check," said Colly. "Then maybe we can avoid a
party like the one we had on the stone-barge. If a
squad of cops come in swinging lathis, at a time we
fix beforehand after we case the joint—"

"Yes. Leave that to me. After you have gone I will
not leave this telephone. Tell me exactly where and
when you want the police, and how many. Give me
twenty-four hours' notice if you can. Then you are
setting a trap at the same time as you are walking
into the trap. I shall have a word with our friend in
Delhi."

"Do we make our number with the local cops when
we get there?"

"No. Leave it entirely to me."

"I've been here before," said Veena suddenly in
English. She had not spoken a word of English for
two weeks, and had hardly heard one.

"No, dear Veena," said Kashi. "I know for a fact
that you have never been here."

Veena looked from the bullock cart out across the
swampland at the edge of Bombay. The swamp was
a city of close-packed little huts. Among the huts
smoked thousands of cooking fires; among them
twined a network of shallow open drains. It was in-
humanly squalid, far below the point to which human beings could sink and retain any self-respect
at all.

Veena looked at the bustee huts with remembered horror. "Yes," she insisted, speaking meekly as she knew she must speak, but sure that she was right. "I remember the huts. I remember that smell. Yes, I *clearly* remember that smell. I remember . . ."

"Yes?"

"Colly. Sandro."

"What is that? Colisandro? Is that a place?"

"I don't know," said Veena truthfully. "It just came into my head. Is it one word or two? I don't know."

Kashi said later to Lal. Chand, "Sheelah should be whipped with a wire rope. The memory begins to return. When the goat sees the tiger it may try to bite through its tether and run."

"That we can prevent."

"Oh yes."

Sandro and Colly went from Benares to Bombay, from Bombay to Aurangabad. They travelled publicly and comfortably. They did not have to take deliberate pains to be seen; it was enough not to take pains not to be seen. The trap, if there was a trap, must be there for them, or they would never again see the bait.

Ajanta or Ellora. The places not dissimilar, about fifty miles apart, set in steep hillsides above the huge plain of the Deccan.

"Seems both are strings of caves," said Colly.

"Strings of traps," said Sandro cheerfully. His cheerfulness was only partly assumed. The prospect of action after the agony of enforced idleness raised his spirits.

Ajanta or Ellora. It was tempting to go one each to each place, but the idea was no sooner mooted than dismissed. They must stay together. There was an outside chance that the telephone message from the unknown informer was a true bill: that the caller had been shocked by Jenny's abduction, or for some other reason was double-crossing the abductors: that she was alive, and would be at one or other holy place, and could be rescued.

Seven days had passed since the telephone call. If the caller was both well intentioned and well informed, Jenny would be at either Ajanta or Ellora in the next few days: on any day, and at one place or the other.

They decided to go to Ajanta first, on the arbitrary ground that the temples there were older.

They had not expected, in their preoccupation, to be stunned either by natural beauty or by archaeological fascination. But Ajanta was stunning. It was set in hills so dominating the great plain that, although they were nearly on the western side of India, the rivers all ran eastwards, hundreds of miles across the plains into the Pacific. A river variously called the Vagha or Waghora—on maps of different ages— tumbled in a series of spectacular waterfalls down a gorge in the face of the hills. From the river precipitous cliffs rose to dense woods, the colour and texture of broccoli; along the face of the cliffs, curving with their curves, ran a broad ledge; behind the ledge were the important pillared entrances of the caves.

They were very fine: a community of associated Buddhist monasteries, with living quarters, caves of assembly, caves of worship. The temple caves were heavily decorated with the familiar, heavy, fatly-smiling person of the Buddha. Many of the carvings were brightly painted, and many of the walls covered with complicated tempera paintings on thick layers of plaster.

It was pitch dark in the caves. From the roofs of some hung bats in untidy clumps. A hundred kidnapped girls could have lain, tied up and gagged, in each cave, with a regiment of assassins hiding behind each one; except that parties of tourists were being shown round by eager, conscientious official guides, each of whom carried a powerful electric arc-light. The lights were very bright. They swept everywhere, in every corner, exploring every inch of the elaborate decorations, every niche, cranny, cell, couch, shelf.

Colly and Sandro joined three successive parties of tourists. They saw the whole of all the caves. They saw vast areas of peaceful, happy, uninhibited paintings, thousands of benign statues. There was no Jenny. There was no trap. There was no faint possibility of a trap here. It must have been obvious to the enemy that they would go only where there was light: and that where there was light there was also a crowd of people.

"The other dump," said Colly, "will have to be a little different if they're gonna try jumping us."

From a distance it looked remarkably similar. Once again steep mountains dominated the enormous plain, and waterfalls curved out of cliffs into a lush valley. Once again caves gaped from a path traversing the mountainside. The scale was grander. Huge entrances had been carved out of the living rock, pillars, stairways, the figures of gods and beasts; behind the entrances, some of the caves had upper storeys and balconies and cloisters and colonnades carved out of the basalt rock of the mountain.

When they came up to the caves from the open

valley below they saw that there were differences: important differences.

Ellora was a more wearisome drive than Ajanta from any place with good air-conditioned hotels, so there were far fewer tourists. Perhaps as a result the guides were fewer, lazier, less helpful. Since much of the carving could be seen without electric light, lamps were not in constant use, so that there were many large areas always in the obscurity of complicated shadow, in near darkness or pitch darkness. Ellora had not merely caves but also the amazing temple of Kailasa, the image of Shiva's heaven recreated on earth, a place of unimaginable origin, a place that might have been designed by gods or demons for a fatal game of hide-and-seek. There were Buddhist and Jain caves at Ellora, but the bulk of the place and its heart were Hindu. Tourists might go to Ajanta to stare; pilgrims came to Ellora to worship. To worship what? Among the bland gods and the laughing gods and the little goddesses of heartbreaking beauty, among the buttocks and breasts and curious copulations, were to be seen, here and there, reminders of terror and death in the dreadful person of Kali.

An official with more chins than manners approached Colly and Sandro. He said that they might not take photographs, or make drawings, without a written permit obtainable from Hyderabad; this would take a few days or perhaps weeks and would entail the payment of five rupees.

Sandro said they had no cameras. Colly said they did not know how to draw.

They agreed to inspect the unlikely before they looked at the likely, as a huntsman in cold-scenting country makes good the ground behind him before he casts his hounds forward. They went first to the southern end of the escarpment and looked quickly at the twelve Buddhist caves which had replaced the temples of Ajanta. The atmosphere was peaceful, almost indolent. There was no sense of threat. They thought there would be nothing for them in the Buddhist caves; there was nothing. They went to the Jain caves, five of them, more than a mile away along the escarpment to the north. Still the atmosphere was amiable, obtrusively harmless, as might be expected in the shrines of a sect who breathe always through gauze so as not to kill by mistake the smallest gnat or microbe. The Jain caves were entirely deserted except for carved gods, and hundreds of naked male effigies, and flying foxes which squealed like pigs and flapped like umbrellas and caused even Sandro to blink and recoil.

They came to the Kailasa, the Hindu centre.

"My God," said Colly, after a long time.

They had known what to expect, but it was more than anyone could have expected. When the Hindus of the eighth century decided, or were guided, into establishing a great temple at this place, they embarked on the task downwards instead of upwards. They excavated an immense hole in the ground, leaving in the middle of the hole a lump of rock of prodigious size. They carved at that lump until they had removed what they did not want: and what was left was a massive and elaborate temple, crawling with sculpture, chambered, crannied, pillared, here and there in bright sunlight and here and there as dark as the depths of the caves.

The sculpture almost writhed with vitality. Only the life-sized elephants were peaceful. Animals and gods fought and fornicated. Naked lovers, opulent, shameless, demonstrated a hundred varieties of the impossible. Shiva had twelve arms. Kali was a skeleton, yet even she was grinningly alive; even the skulls of her necklace were alive, and the snakes which made her girdle, and the two dying men on whom she rested.

Among all the beasts and breasts and laughter, this was the Kali of Kalighat with the terrified sacrificial goats and the frothing, hysterical worshippers; this was the nasty little black goddess of Bindachun with the blank and terrifying silver-disc eyes and the incongruous garlands of flowers.

"Like coming home," murmured Colly.

Sandro nodded.

Now, here, the sense of threat seemed to writhe out of the writhing, naked stone bodies, to beat dark leathery wings at their faces like the bats and flying foxes, to grin like the skullface of Kali and the skulls of her necklace.

"This is the place," said Sandro. "*Oggi, domani, forse doppodomani . . .*"

Kashi, called Feringhia, rested in Khultabad, on the hilltop above the sacred caves. He stayed in the house of a Muslim. This was no oddity: for he and his host talked in the language Ramasi, and were evidently in some sort brothers.

Messages were brought.

Veena, in the next room, saw the messengers but did not hear the messages, which were delivered in Ramasi to Feringhia and his Muslim brother and their friends.

There was much discussion of the omens for the morrow.

The atmosphere was one of sober joy, of excitement kept in check by that sense of good form which controls serious men while they prepare for a religious observance.

* * *

Ishur Ghose said that everything was ready, that the warning orders had been issued and acknowledged. Two truckloads of policemen, under at least one senior officer, were ready to embus at short notice. The police were thankful to have the chance to help rescue Lady Jennifer; and they were excited that there might be some lead to the hundreds of mysterious disappearances.

"Two o'clock tomorrow afternoon," said Colly. "Fourteen hundred hours. The Temple of Kailasa. The more the better."

"Wilco."

Fourteen

Purohit was pleased with his new job, which had been procured for him by the friend of a cousin of a friend of his sister. He was a fat little man, not energetic, constantly worried about his health; he was sure the quiet of the countryside was good for him after the noise of Bombay, which made sleep so difficult in the daytime. He liked to make sure of plenty of sleep. He believed it was as necessary to his health as was abstinence from sex and the regular giving of alms. If he got enough sleep—twenty hours in the twenty-four—he thought his health could survive the giving of fewer alms.

Purohit had been appointed an official guide at Ellora. He wore a uniform. He had status, authority, and a few tips. Not many tips because not many visitors. More visitors would have meant more money but less sleep. Every coin had two sides. A living wage was enough. If more money meant continual wakefulness it was too dearly bought.

Purohit dozed in the gigantic portico of the Temple of Kailasa. A small party of men strolled past him into the temple. He opened one eye and at once closed it again. The men were bare-footed, in dhotis. They did not want a guide. They were pilgrims, not tourists: poor farmers, good for a few annas at most.

Sometime later (Purohit could not have told how

much later) another party went quietly into the temple; a woman as well as a dozen men; perhaps two dozen. They were of the same useless sort as the first party, not inclined to ask for information about the temple from the dog-eared official booklet, not inclined to disturb Purohit at all. The woman was heavily veiled. The men surrounded her. It seemed that they conveyed her, or convoyed her, into the temple. A flicker of curiosity disturbed the dead midday calm of Purohit's mind; but it died at once of fatigue. He resumed his doze.

After another period of healthful repose Purohit heard the ominous sound of a car. People who came in cars were another matter. They were restless and greedy for facts, Indians as well as Europeans. The high-caste Indians were much more shocked by some of the carvings than the Europeans, but some of the Europeans were shocked too. Europeans walked faster and tipped better; as always advantage was weighed against disadvantage.

The noise of the car grew louder. Purohit sighed. He raised one heavy eyelid. He saw the car stop. It was very dusty from the roads. Two men got out, whom he recognized. They were making a second visit. They were gluttons for punishment. They were foreign-side gentlemen, but one looked like an Indian except for his hair, which curled, his eyes, which were blue, and his size, which was more that of a buffalo than of a man. Purohit had attended them yesterday. He winced at the memory. They had tipped him but they had kept him awake and on his feet for three hours. It had been a terrible afternoon. Now it was only mid-morning. Maybe they would stay all day. The thought was appalling. Purohit shuddered at the threat to his delicate health.

The Europeans looked round slowly. They saw no

one because there was no one to be seen, except the chief guide, whose manner was deliberately calculated to reduce the number of visitors. Even Purohit, who sympathised with his objectives, deplored his methods. The Europeans turned their backs on the chief guide, who officiously advanced; they spoke to each other for a short time. Purohit, having opened his other eye, observed them with foreboding. He hoped they would go to the Buddhist caves or the Jain caves (none of which Purohit, himself, had ever considered visiting) but they came inexorably towards him.

He stood up, settled his cap straighter on his brow, and shuffled towards them. The smaller European smiled and greeted him in Urdu. Purohit replied in the English which had got him the job: he urged that another day, a less hot day, would be better for the visitors. They ignored this kindly-meant suggestion. They strolled through the massive pillared portico, past its statued guardians, and on into the glaring sunlight which surrounded the temple. Purohit was obliged to follow them.

He noticed, as he did so, that another party of humble men had materialised near the portico. They had perhaps come down the track from Khultabad. There were eight or ten of them, poor farmers, young men. Purohit stood aside to let them go ahead of him into the temple, as they were in some sort his guests: but they smiled and indicated that they would stay where they were just outside the entrance. Perhaps they wanted to admire the view over the Deccan plain, or rest before they went into the temple, or eat. They squatted on the ground, forming what was almost a kind of cordon across the entrance to the temple. It occurred to Purohit that their presence might deter other visitors. He was grateful to them. He might, because they were there, the sooner resume his needful sleep.

Inside the enormous crater where stood the temple, some of the earlier visitors were looking at the carvings, squatting, praying. A few were apparently asleep, incurring Purohit's helpless envy. The majority were not to be seen. The woman was not to be seen. It was not surprising. They might be worshipping in the innermost shrine of Shiva, or anywhere among the complicated glooms of the temple.

Purohit bestirred himself. He followed the Europeans and asked how he might be of service to them.

"Of course," said Lal Chand. "The omens are favourable, and we have no choice but to kill him as well as the others."

"A religious mendicant?" said Sanghavi, shocked. "Have you forgotten what happened to our forefathers when they transgressed the laws of the Goddess?"

"He is a guide in the employ of the government."

"That also, but the other also. He is begging. Look. He approaches the Frankish persons. His hand is stretched out for alms."

"But he is not a *religious* beggar."

"Not religious? A servant of this temple?"

"I do not *think* the words of the law as we know the law were intended to apply to such as he. We must ask the Jemadar."

They faced the Jemadar with the dilemma. He agreed that it was a nice point. Watching from the shadow of a statue of the lovely goddess Sarasvati, he acknowledged the justice of Sanghavi's point that the guide was continually stretching his palm for charity. But was it charity? Was he not offering himself for hire? A religious mendicant was certainly in

one of the categories which the brotherhood was forbidden to strangle. The issue was debated seriously,
without haste. There was plenty of time. Lal Chand
did not make the point that the guide, if not killed
with the others, prevented their death by the incon-
venient fact of his presence; this point was in all
minds, but it was not relevant to the central issue
under discussion.

The Jemadar at length judged that a uniformed
guide to the temple, beg he never so assiduously, was
clearly to be distinguished from a saddhu or any
other renouncer of the world. The Goddess would
condone the sacrifice.

It was a fortunate chance that the party included
three brothers with the rank of Strangler.

Veena waited for the signal. As soon as she saw it
she would begin the diverting game in which Kashi
had instructed her. It was a form of worship at the
same time, no less pleasing to the Goddess for being
enjoyable, like immersion in Gunga on a hot day.

Veena was to sob and moan and feign sickness. The
more convincing her distress the more pleasing to
the Goddess. She might laugh in her heart—Kashi,
smiling, assured her that she might do so—but the
face she showed to the temple must be stricken with
anguish.

Could she do it? Was Kashi right to trust her with
so important a pujah? Veena assured him that he
was right, that she would feign such misery as would
melt the stony hearts of the very statues.

Veena convinced him and the others that she could
do it, that she would enjoy doing it. This was something she knew, even though she knew nothing about
herself. Play-acting came naturally to her. If sobbing
were called for she would sob, if laughter laugh.

She squatted now, in the most normal position of all poor Indians, in the deep shadow cast by two Homeric stone lovers; the breasts of the woman were larger than footballs, her buttocks than the great rubber balls thrown by rich children on the beach. Her waist was tiny. Her face showed a placid acceptance of the amazing things her lover was doing to her.

Veena did not think Kashi would do such things to her.

"It is as we expected," murmured Lal Chand. "They expect trouble. They are on the alert. See. They give the appearance of being absorbed in looking at the sacred carvings, but it is never more than one who looks at carvings. The other looks everywhere else. See also that they never go very near any dark place, and that they look round each corner from a distance before they go round it. Even in this place they make it impossible for a man to jump out at them, to take them by surprise."

"And they are doubtless armed."

"Yes. We know that they have knives and little clubs. We guess that they have guns."

"The tethered goat will draw the eye of the tiger when it bleats."

"Now?"

"Soon."

Purohit's function was to provide, for a discretionary reward, such information as visitors might require and as he could find in the little book with which he had been issued. This was all his function. It was not part of his duties to succour the sick or comfort the despairing. In the streets of Bombay he would have walked past a man fallen in a fit, or a man knocked over by a car; in the Kailasa Temple he ignored the agonised sobs of the woman. His dharma, his sacred duty, lay not in helping her but in other things. It might be somebody's business to help her but it was not Purohit's.

He walked away, more briskly than usual, from the woman sprawled and blubbering behind the gigantic lovers. He rejoined the Europeans, and began giving them unsolicited information about the two-headed beasts and three-hooded snakes of the carvings. His smooth, insistent, monotonous voice drowned the distant sobbing of the woman. Purohit hoped that she would soon stop, or go away, or die.

"That is a *bad* man," murmured Lal Chand. "He should at least have gone to look at a young woman in such evident distress."

"Then we could have killed him quickly and concentrated on the others."

"Yes. What a *bad* man, simply to walk away."

"How many guys do you count?" asked Colly, appearing to give his full attention to a broken carving of a lotus flower.

"Nine. Ten. Eleven."

"Yeah. How many more you can't see?"

"It would be interesting to know. It is an interesting speculation."

"Nothing like a little interesting speculation to pass the time. Ah, Christ, here's gabby come back to tell us a naked woman doesn't have a sari on."

Veena saw the signal that told her to weep more loudly. Evidently, for an inscrutable reason, the Goddess wanted a louder noise of lamentation. It was all right with Veena. She grinned quickly: then, remembering Kashi's most strict instructions, she contorted

her features into a babyish mask of misery. She began
to wail like a tomcat.

The reason for her own performance, the need
for such nonsense, was completely baffling to her.
But it was not surprising. In her new life she had
learned not to be surprised by anything, because everything was at once astonishing and normal.

All that troubled her were unbidden words and
pictures gatecrashing the doors of her mind, intrud-
ing, disturbing: *revenants* from a barely-glimpsed
past which Kashi said had been obliterated by her
illness. It was not quite obliterated. Veena saw misty
treetops and crags, far away, above the blanket of
fog; names, like insects, buzzed in through cracks and
circled meaninglessly inside her skull.

Veena wished they would go away and leave her
in peace. Meanwhile, drowning unwelcome echoes, she
wailed and choked and blubbered with gleeful aban-
don.

"What's that?" murmured Colly. "Some kind of
animal? Could that be a signal?"

The uniformed guide babbled on in his glib, almost meaningless English. Sandro raised an enormous
hand to gesture him to silence. His voice petered out,
and in the silence could be heard, from almost 100
yards away at the other end of the temple, the muf-
fled, anguished cries of a woman.

Sandro seemed inclined to forget all prudence, to
run like a mad bull immediately to the sound.

"Hold it, boy," murmured Colly urgently. "Gabby's
here. Let's use him."

Sandro nodded.

He produced, idly, a handful of rupees from his
pocket. He told the fat little guide to see who was
crying, and why, and having seen to return at once.

To Purohit the money put a different complexion on the whole matter. It was not his dharma to behave like a medical orderly; it was his dharma to earn money from tourists.

He stretched out a tentative palm.

The dark-skinned buffalo with blue eyes indicated with word and gesture that the money was his when he returned with information about the woman and her trouble.

Purohit began to argue the point, which was to him an interesting one. The man like a buffalo used stronger words and clearer gestures. Purohit shrugged, smiled self-deprecatingly, and shuffled away.

Through copious crocodile tears Veena saw the uniformed guide trotting towards her. She wondered why he had not done so before. He stopped with his sandalled feet inches from her head. He looked down at her with distaste on his spherical brown face. He said something in a language which Veena did not understand; then asked her in English why she was making such a din on government property.

One of Kashi's friends materialised behind the guide. He asked someone invisible for a cigarette. Veena felt another unusual start of surprise: it had not occurred to her that devout people would smoke cigarettes in so holy a place as this.

The response was not a cigarette but something so terrible, so unthinkable, that it could not be happening. Another of Kashi's friends darted out from behind a massive pillar and bowled the fat little guide over onto his face. Two more descended on him as, in another life, Veena had seen terriers descend on a badger. In the twinkling of an eye a fourth crouched by the guide's shoulders with a length of yellow and white cotton in his hands. Veena's senses reeled as the cotton was whisked round the man's neck, and twisted and tightened so as to cut off his single gargling cry almost before he began to make it.

Veena screamed. She knew what she was seeing. The word 'Thug' came into her head: a word never used to her by Kashi or his friends, a word out of the past, out of something long ago learned, out of a picture blinked onto the screen of her mind by a subconscious projector.

Veena screamed again. The fat little guide was dead. That was horribly obvious. He lay like a sack. The men who had killed him glanced at her. Their faces were serious but serene. They did not mind her screaming. They even expected her to scream, and were not dissatisfied with her performance. It came to Veena that this was a continuation of the game of feigned tears. The tears and wails had brought the guide, brought him to be killed. She had brought him to be killed. She had helped kill him. This was the pujah. Thugs. Kali. Goats. Blood. Colisandro. Kashi. Kashi before the shrine of Kali, Kashi with the blood of the sacrificial goat almost splashing his feet. Her Kashi, gentle Kashi, worshipping at the feet of the dreadful goddess.

All around her the enormous statues writhed with satanic vitality. They were evil and perverse. Their smiles were false. The opulent, naked, contorted lovers were hatching more cruelty, more crime.

Veena knew with utter certainty that all this was foreign to her: she did not belong to it: she was no part of it nor it of her. The coffee-brown arm that she could see supporting herself was not her arm. The black hair that fell across her screaming face from below her veil was not her hair. Veena was not her name. Kashi was not her lover.

It was the only world she knew, and she had thankfully embraced it in her confusion, and it was false. She had been cheated, tricked. She had been hoodwinked into helping these little brown murderers. She was suddenly beside herself with anger.

She scrambled to her feet. Her movements were brusque and Western. She began to shout, not knowing what she was shouting. A hand went over her mouth. Hands pinned her arms to her sides. She struggled violently. She bit the hand on her mouth. It shot away. She shouted again, words chosen for her by memory, by something inside herself she did not know. The hand or another hand was clamped over her face. Though she struggled she was held fast. She was too angry to be frightened.

Colly and Sandro heard the sobbing wailing cease. They glanced at each other, then continued to look alertly round. Colly had given up all pretence of scrutinising the broken lotus flower. The men that they could see, the dozen insignificant figures in dhotis or shabby trousers, seemed also to be alert. They had heard the sobbing and the end of the sobbing. They had not moved but they were all on their feet.

There was a curious, ugly sound as of a man gargling with treacle.

A woman screamed, and again.

This time Colly looked inclined to dash without hesitation or precaution to the place. Sandro gestured downwards with the flat of his hand.

Sandro said, "That is maybe Jenny. We cannot help her if we are dead."

"The guide's dead."

"Yes, I think."

The dozen inconspicuous men in the shadows of

the cavern about the temple still stood, alert as jackals, watching and waiting.

The shout came in a clear, high, angry voice: "Foul!"

They knew the voice. There was no mistaking it.

"She's okay," muttered Colly. "Sounds mad."

"Yes. Wait."

The shout rang again along the echoing, writhing immensities of the temple: "Mayday! Mayday! Mayday! May—"

The voice was cut off. Dead silence filled the huge crater in the mountainside.

Getting to Jenny meant passing a dozen men that they could see, an unknown number in the shadows and crannies of the temple. Helping her meant looking at her and not elsewhere; using hands for her and not for weapons.

"Whose move?" asked Collie chattily.

"They have never killed a woman," said Sandro. "Not one. It is maybe their rule."

"I don't believe," said Colly, "we should count on them keeping any rules."

"They do not use weapons."

"Same comment to that, chum."

"Yes. I do not know whose move. Maybe ours. Or maybe there is no move. Maybe nothing happens until two o'clock, when the police come."

"That's too much to hope for."

"Yes."

"They are quite unnatural," said Lal Chand. "They are perfect pigs. They are as bad as the guide. A poor young lady screams for help and they stand as still as this stone."

"Yes. It is time we moved them. Lift Veena to her

feet. Be careful not to hurt her. So. Hold tight. I wonder why she is struggling. Do you not trust me, Veena? Now the rope. Put the end over the leg of that woman who is being ravished. How curious that such a thing should be useful as a gallows. I venture to think Bhowani would enjoy the irony. Now the noose. Pull it tight. Not too tight, fool. You are sure that her wrists are tied firmly behind her? And the ankles together? I hope it is not hurting her much, but I am afraid it must be uncomfortable. So. Listen to me, Veena. Can you hear me? Silly child, the gag is not covering your ears, of course you hear and understand. You are to stand on this spot. If you let yourself collapse I am afraid you will hang yourself. Do you understand that? We shall not do it. We should hate to do such a thing, and besides our laws expressly forbid it. You are quite safe from any violence from us. But of course we cannot prevent you from committing suicide, if that is what you wish to do. If you try to move away, or fall over, or throw yourself sideways, or collapse, you will hang yourself. I am saving your life, as our law requires, by telling you this. There is no need for you to be hurt in the smallest degree. The only way you will be hurt is if you hurt yourself. See, she understands. Good girl. Stand quite still exactly where you are and no harm will come to you. Pull the rope tight over that disgraceful leg. Not too tight, fool. Do you think I intend to marry a corpse? There. Perfect. I do not think we shall be here much longer."

Fifteen

The girl was a hundred yards away. The lower part of her face was veiled. The veil might have concealed a gag. Her brow and cheeks were dark brown. The small amount of hair visible was blue-black and straight. She wore a sari and an enveloping shawl round her shoulders and over her head. Heavy gold ornaments, rings and bangles, winked in the sunshine against dark bare arms and ankles. She stood erect, motionless, silent, anonymous, with a rope round her neck.

There was no possibility of recognising a veiled brown girl a hundred yards away. But neither man was in the smallest doubt about who she was. As though by telepathy, as though by magic, distance was abolished and disguise lifted off. A wordless greeting throbbed through the glaring sunlight: an appeal: a warning.

The rope went from her neck to the jutting, massive leg of an abandoned stone woman sprawling in erotic ecstasy on a nine-foot statuary tableau. The rope hung loosely between the living neck and the almost-living stone leg. Somebody held the other end: somebody hidden by another statue, in cover and in deep shadow.

The rope tautened. It ran as straight as an arrow from the girl's neck to the dimpled stone knee of the carving. The girl stood stock still. Of course she had been told to do so. Of course her life depended on doing so.

She was about to be hanged before their eyes.

"Our move," said Colly.

She saw two Europeans in tropical clothes, a hundred yards away, near the far end of the temple, six yards from the side of the temple.

As soon as she saw them her heart leapt the hundred yards over the dusty stone floor of the cavern, through the sun-cooked and insect-haunted air, along the pagan monstrosities of the temple carvings. Her heart leapt to the two men because she knew that they were hers and she theirs.

She knew suddenly that she was European, not Indian; Christian, not Hindu; white, not brown. Kashi had lied. Her brown skin and black hair, her name and language were lies. Kashi had deceived her and used her, and was using her still as bait to catch and kill her real people, her real loves.

Jenny knew she was Jenny.

Two things had jerked her violently into self-knowledge. The first was the murder in front of her eyes of the fat little temple guide. They thought it would be acceptable to her as it was acceptable to them, but it filled her with horror and repugnance, and with rage at being tricked and deceived. The second thing was Kashi, whom she had esteemed and trusted, himself supervising the placing of the noose about her neck.

Meanwhile the noose was there. It was tight. It did not immediately threaten to choke her. She could not get her chin inside the noose. Her wrists were tied behind her back. She was completely help-

less, and at the mercy of the man holding the end
of the rope.

Had she been what for weeks she thought she was,
she would have accepted the position passively, trustingly, without fear. Veena the Rajasthani girl was
ruled by fatalism. But she had been shocked into
awareness; she felt anger and she felt fear. For the
first time she was badly frightened, for her friends
and for herself.

"First we get a little more near," said Sandro con-
versationally, as though he had seen a new statue
that mildly interested him. "I go in front, you cover
my back."

"I don't believe you're gonna shoot through that
rope," said Colly.

"No. But the rope goes to a hand. I will not see
the head of the man whose hand it is, but I will
maybe know where is that head. He will be looking
out over that stone. It is not possible that he will
stand so that he cannot see us. Nobody would stand
so."

"He may be a tall guy or a short guy."

"I do not care if I hit him in the eye or in the
throat."

They began to stroll, gently, parallel to the side
of the temple. They kept well away from the deep,
complicated shadows in which could be concealed so
many men. Both had their weapons ready but concealed.

Sandro's eyes flickered between Jenny and the invisible end of the rope. He measured angles and prob-
abilities. He had to make the assumption that the
man holding the rope was right-handed, and that he
had his right hand on the rope to hold it taut and
the other hand nearby to take Jenny's weight if she

was to be hanged. If the man had been wearing a white turban Sandro would perhaps have seen it, but he was evidently bareheaded and his dark face and hair were invisible. There was no gleam of eyeballs or of teeth.

Sandro trusted Colly to look everywhere else, at the men behind them and for signs of men invisible in the temple.

Sandro came unhurriedly on. He looked relaxed, almost sleepy, but he was wound to a pitch of the most intense concentration and alertness. He was no more than thirty yards from Jenny, who was as motionless as any of the statues behind her. He was twenty-five yards away: and twenty. There was no movement visible in the temple. There was no guessing how many men were there, or where they were.

The men behind them had advanced with them. There were four men not ten yards from Colly, seven more a little behind them, others in the remoter glooms of the edge of the cavern. Colly's hand rested casually inside his light cotton coat. He walked backwards, his back almost touching Sandro's.

Jenny did not move. She could not move. Sandro saw unfamiliar black eyes fixed unwinkingly on his face.

Suddenly Jenny's chin jerked upwards. The rope had been tightened. She was standing on tiptoe. The extra height was not enough. Her chin was still being hauled upwards and her head twisted on her neck.

Sandro was certain the man holding the rope now had both hands to it. He must be taking some of Jenny's weight on the rope. The pressure of the rope on her neck must be tremendous. It did not immediately threaten to kill her, but a small extra pull would kill her. The man must have two hands on the rope and he must be in a position to see Jenny. His head, part of his head, must be clear of the lump of carved basalt rock behind which he was hidden.

A shot might be the spark in the powder-keg.

Let it be. Let the bomb go up.

"Attenzione," Sandro murmured to Colly.

"Feel free," said Colly.

Sandro drew the .38 from the holster under his left armpit. He got off three quick shots in a close pattern round a line which he continued with his eye from the visible line of the rope.

There was a squeal.

Sandro thought he had hit a knuckle or taken off the end of a finger. He had not killed the man.

The rope went slack.

Jenny dived and rolled over, pulling the rope with her. The end of the rope came blessedly into Sandro's view, trailing in the brilliant sunlight over the quarried floor of the cavern.

Faces appeared, moving in the shadows of the temple, eyeballs and a flutter of white cotton clothing. Sandro got off two more quick shots to discourage assault. He did not expect to hit anyone; as far as he knew he did not do so.

Colly was in a crouch immediately behind Sandro, his back to Sandro's back. His gun was in his hand. He traversed it backwards and forwards between the nearest men. They could rush him. There were enough of them. Colly could not kill them all. But he could kill some if they rushed: two or four or six. This was as obvious to them as to Colly. They were brave but they were not suicidal. Every second that went by made them less likely to rush. They might have done so the moment Sandro fired his first shots. But the longer they waited the more time they had to consider how many of them would be killed, and which.

Jenny rolled almost to Sandro's feet. Sandro transferred the gun to his left hand. Without taking his eyes off the temple he reached out his right hand to Jenny. He grabbed her right arm above the elbow, and dragged her, on her side, ten yards further from the temple. He knew it must be painful for Jenny being dragged over the rough stone in her thin sari.

Colly came with him, still crouching, moving crablike over the ground.

Sandro pulled out a knife and clicked open the spring-loaded blade. He allowed himself a split-second glance at the knots on Jenny's wrists. He sliced very carefully through the bonds; the knife was extremely sharp and he did not want to cut off one of Jenny's thumbs. But he did not dare take his eyes from the temple for more than a fraction of a second at a time.

He felt Jenny's hands come free. He felt her take the knife. With the edge of his vision he saw her cut away the cords that tied her ankles. Then she pulled off her gag.

It occurred to Sandro that any other woman he knew would have taken off the gag first.

"Hullo, darling," said Jenny.

"*Ciao*," said Sandro. "*Come stai?*"

"A bit confused. The wrong colour, surely? With the wrong friends?"

"Oh yes, a little wrong."

"A little wrong," echoed Colly. "Keep trying to kill us, to mention one thing I can't like about them. Try as I may I can't like it."

"We have improved the odds," said Sandro. "Can you walk, *tesoro?*"

"Me?" said Jenny. "Yes."

"Okay. We go very carefully to the edge, to the

big wall of the mountain. I will be happy to have
a million tons of rock behind my back. In the dark
maybe we move, but in the light that is the place
to be."

Alert, guns ready, they moved to the edge of the
cavern. Jenny came with them, stiff from being tied
and sore from being dragged over the rock.

"Now tell," said Sandro.

Jenny told how she had been born, without memory or identity, as an Indian in an Indian family,
engaged to be married to an Indian who was a leader
of their enemies.

"Of the Thugs," said Colly.

"Yes. Kashi is Feringhia, and he is a Jemadar of
Thugs. His village and his friends are Thugs. They
speak the language Ramasi. I was to be the mother
of Thugs. The old Thugs were never quite destroyed.
They brought trouble on themselves by breaking the
laws of Kali, especially by killing women. I have
heard all this again and again. A few survived, women
with unborn babies. They waited for a sign. I don't
know what sign. A sign came. It came with an old
man who was important in the government. He is
a leader of them all, I think. I don't know who he
is. They never say his name. Am I speaking in a funny
way? Is English my right language? I'm very mixed
up and scared. My hair is not this colour, is it? My
arms? My fingernails? Are we going to be killed when
it gets dark?"

Colly said slowly, "Yes, baby, but let's go back a
little. A sign that restarted this whole deal came with
—what was it you said?—an old man who was important in the government."

"Yes. A great scholar, a reader of old books."

"Ishur Ghose."

"No," said Sandro, "Ishur Ghose was a senior government agent, and for very many years a great man . . ."

"Kashi is a great man," said Jenny. "Everybody trusts him and goes to him for advice." She added, "He's very nice to his mother. He was very nice to me."

"But—"

"I did not learn much about them but I learned some things. That was when I knew they were special, different, but before I knew they were Thugs. I learned that they have many brothers in the police and the government."

"Ah," said Colly, "that's exactly how we figured it."

"And like a big spider in the middle—" said Sandro.

"Ishur Ghose. I don't believe it yet, but it has to be true. We really must get out of here and tell some cops. Otherwise the whole goddam thing just goes on."

"I think the cops will not believe a word," said Sandro. "They believe like all others the Thugs were destroyed. They go to Jenny's friends, who are most respectable and have wonderful alibis. They do not find anything in writing because there is not anything. They go to Ishur Ghose, who laughs. He is believed, naturally he is believed. We have invented a big slander about India. There are maybe dacoits and burglars and swindlers and murderers but there are not Thugs, not for 130 years."

"So no cops come at two o'clock," said Colly.

"No."

"And five hours after that it gets dark."

"Yes."

"And then we're in a little trouble."

"Yes," agreed Sandro, smiling without humour.

* * *

Sanghavi had been roughly bandaged with a strip of cotton. It was an ugly little wound and had bled profusely. It was very painful. At the same time Sanghavi recognised that he was very lucky. The bullet might well have been destined for his head or heart, but it was written that it should only strike the joint of his thumb. This wound should have been foretold by a proper reading of his horoscope; Sanghavi promised himself an interview with the priest who had cast the horoscope only a few weeks before; a money repayment was the least of the reparations the priest would make.

Even Feringhia, who accepted neither excuses nor any weakness, understood that when Sanghavi was shot in the hand he had to let go of the rope that went to Veena's neck. It was highly unfortunate but Sanghavi could not be blamed by any fair-minded man.

They all saw the European cut the knots that bound Veena's wrists, and Veena herself cut the knots that bound her ankles. They saw her take off the gag; they heard her talking in English, although they could not hear what she said.

It was probable that Veena was no longer altogether Veena. As Feringhia said, Sheelah the witch should be whipped with wire for promising something which had not been performed, for taking money, a lot of money, on false pretences.

But night would fall at last, and with it at last the Europeans. Officials would try to turn them out of the temple at a stated time; it was written up on a notice that at six o'clock visitors must leave the temple and the caves. The chief official guide, the one with the face and manners of a hog, would come among them insisting that they leave. They would

lead him into the temple, out of sight, by a strata-
gem, and there kill him. The omens for killing
continued propitious. The chief guide might have collected a number of tips, and also the proportion on
which he doubtless insisted of the tips given to others. It would not be a lot of money but it would be
pleasing to the Goddess and to her servants.

The entrance to the temple would continue to be
guarded by the group of brothers who were stationed
there. They might keep persons out or let them in.
If persons came in they came to their death. No
women would be suffered to come in.

It did not matter if Veena saw more deaths, the
deaths of her one-time friends. She had been adopted
into the brotherhood. She was privy to some of its
secrets; she had been instructed in some matters and
observed others. It was not usual for a woman of the
sect to take part in murders, as Veena had taken part
in the murder of the fat guide, but it was not unheard
of. There was respectable precedent. No laws were
broken.

Veena, of course, was to be recaptured. She might
be and continue defiant, especially if her memory
altogether returned. That was Feringhia's problem.
He said that he was still determined to marry her.
He loved her passionately. It was understandable. She
was very comely and would bear fine sons. She would
never be able to escape. She would be taken back to
the village in Rajasthan and there remain for ever.
She would live and die within the confines of the village and its nearest fields. The whole village would
be her guardian. At the most intimate moments she
would never be unwatched. Everybody in the village
would be totally loyal to Feringhia in that regard
as in all others. Her defiance and enmity might be

disagreeable to Feringhia but they would not affect
her own destiny. That remained fixed.

It was now only a question of waiting until dark,
until the guns of the Europeans became useless. The
big man would take a lot of killing, but there were
a lot of men to kill him.

They waited until the salvation came at two o'clock
which they did not think would come. Two o'clock
came, but no police; two-thirty; three.

It was terribly hot.

Jenny told them as much as she could understand
about what had happened to her. She told them as
much as she had been taught, or had overheard, about
the brotherhood. She knew nothing fundamental, no
philosophy or theology or legend to justify the sect's
grisly form of worship. It had only become clear to
her during the morning that murder was their business. But this realisation made sense of a lot of things
that had baffled her: of the prolonged desertion of
some of the villagers of their farms; of windfalls of
unexpected wealth; of the language Ramasi; of the
nightlong disappearance of Kashi and his friends during the journey to Bombay, and of their sober glee
and jingling pouches in the dawn.

"And the omens," she said. "I didn't understand it
at first. I couldn't think what they were looking for,
listening to. Crows, donkeys, jackals, birds flying or
calling on one side or the other side."

Jenny's English was rapidly becoming English instead of Babu. She was growing back into herself as
she talked, because she was being objective about
things which she had passively accepted.

She said, "Some of the women know about most
of the omens too. They listen for them and report.

Muni used to report to Kashi that she'd seen such and such, and he always trusted her. It didn't make any sense to me but now it does. Once in the village a man's turban fell off into a cooking fire, and they were in a terrible state. They cancelled a journey they were just about to take. I couldn't understand it at all, but I do now. They were going on shikar and the omen was very bad, as bad as could be."

"I wish we could organise something like that," said Colly. "Might send them all scampering home. But I don't see how we light a fire, and having lit a fire I don't see how . . ."

"We could find a lizard," said Jenny.

"Well, yes, we could. I see a few from where I hunker. Do you want a pet, like guys in the Tower of London making friends with rats?"

"A lizard on a man's garment is a bad omen."

"It is? You're sure?"

"Yes."

"How bad?"

"I don't know."

"Bad enough to get them hightailing out of here?"

"I don't know."

"Does it have to be one of their garments, or could it be my garment?"

"One of theirs."

"Sure?"

"No."

"Any special kind of lizard?"

"I don't know."

"Does the lizard have to get there by chance?"

"They wouldn't invite it."

"No, but how about if I threw it? Would that count as the omen?"

"I don't know."

"There's an awful lot of doubts surrounding this. Do you know any more bad omens?"

"No. Just the turban and the lizard."

"We try the lizard," said Sandro.

"Yeah. First catch your lizard. What a way for two grown men and a weird kind of female to spend a long hot day. Then what happens? Do I walk up to a guy intending to drop my lizard on his pants? What happens when he runs away? Do I chase him, waving my lizard like a goddam flag?"

"We shoot a man in the leg," said Sandro.

"Well, yeah. We could do that. Just nail one in the thigh, in cold blood. Then sashay up and drop a lizard, keeping clear of the blood if possible."

"Is crude maybe. Think of another way."

"There's a much better way," said Jenny. "I'll give myself up to them. Surrender to them."

"With a lizard hidden in the folds of that shawl," said Colly. "Yes. But suppose it's not a bad omen if it gets dropped on purpose? Or it's the wrong kind of lizard? Or it's got no hex if a woman's touched it? Or something? Once you get into this tortured oriental superstition area you don't know what to expect. Everything's screwy, nothing's logical. And if the omen doesn't work your way, you're grabbed again, maybe with another rope around your neck—"

"No," said Jenny. "Because I'll have a gun too."

Sixteen

They tried to think of another way.

They sat in the shade at the edge of the cavern, on the roughly-hewn basalt rock of the hollowed-out mountain. A dozen men, squatting, watched them fixedly from thirty and fifty yards away. Many other eyes were no doubt fixed on them from the darkness of the temple. The portico of the cavern was guarded by an unknown number of men; some showed themselves briefly inside the gates but there were doubtless more outside. The Thugs must have taken precautions against interruption.

Eventually the odds would swing against them, inexorably, all the way. When it was full dark they would have no chance at all. Colly and Sandro had foreseen that they were taking a risk of this order, but now they wanted to get out. They had Jenny and they wanted to get her out, and they had from her knowledge which, properly used, might end the murders. They wanted to get the knowledge out and use it.

They tried to think of a way of improving the odds which did not involve Jenny walking back to the Thugs and putting her head into another noose. Gun or no gun, she would be taking an appalling risk. Recapture was the very worst thing that could happen to her. Death was far preferable. They tried to think of a way which did not involve so extreme a risk of her death or recapture; but they failed.

They discussed making a dash for the portico and shooting their way out: but although they did some killing they would be overwhelmed by weight of numbers. They discussed trying to climb onto the squat roof of the temple; but although they might postpone their deaths they would not prevent them. They discussed picking off the men they could see, one by one with bullets; but although they got two or three the rest would simply withdraw out of range or behind cover.

They fixed on Jenny's plan and for a long time they discussed the details.

"First catch your lizard." And catch it without revealing to dozens of watchful eyes that you were catching it.

The lizards were shy; they moved fast and there were thousands of crannies for them to bolt into. Jenny thought the lizard should be alive; it should run across a garment, not simply flop there and lie. Had they been able to go lizard-hunting openly it would not have been easy but it would have been easier, but the Thugs might guess correctly what they wanted with a lizard. While they were hunting they had to be, themselves, as alert as the lizards: they had to continue to watch, ceaselessly, the men they could see and the shadows of the temple and the portico. For three full hours they concentrated totally on catching a lizard, undamaged, without giving away what they were doing, and without being caught off their guard. Again and again the flicker of a tail in a cranny just eluded their fingertips. They almost despaired.

Then a lizard ran across Colly's trouser-leg and he grabbed it. He held it gently, hiding it in his lap.

It looked at him with expressionless black eyes from a tiny, wrinkled face. It was a small and inexperienced lizard, blackish for camouflage on the rock.

Very, very carefully, hiding what they were doing, they transferred the lizard from Colly's keeping to Jenny's. She held it safely under her shawl. Colly gave her his gun. She held that also.

Then they began to quarrel.

The brothers, watching from the shadows of the temple, wondered what the mad Europeans were doing. They were killing insects: perhaps fleas. Veena also. It did not matter. It was mysterious but without importance.

Now they sat discoursing. The voices were audible but not the words. Then the voices were a little raised. The discourse became a dispute. Veena moved a little away from the two men. They were arguing with her. First one and then the other made an impassioned speech. She answered in a low voice, turning her face away.

At last Veena stood up. She spoke to the men loudly and clearly, in English. Most of the brothers understood what she said.

Veena said, "No. You are wrong. You judge without understanding. I thought you were my friends but you are my enemies. There are my friends."

They saw Veena gesture with her chin towards the temple: towards themselves. Her hands were under her shawl, as though she clutched her breast, as though she were in pain. It was not surprising, after the brutal way in which she had been dragged across the rock.

She cried, "They were not going to kill me. They would never do so. You do not understand our law. You do not understand anything about us. You will be killed. I shall watch. If I am told to I shall help."

She turned and walked slowly towards the temple.

"A trick," murmured someone.

"No. She would not dare. She would not come back to us alone."

"The Jemadar says she is brave and clever."

"If this is a trick she is brave but she is not clever."

Veena stopped five yards from the temple. She called, "Kashi?"

"Yes."

"I have returned. Do you not greet me?"

"I greet you, Veena. Come into the temple."

"No. I obey you in everything but not in that. I do not wish to come to the place where the man was strangled. I do not think I should look on such things, not yet. I do not trust my courage. Do not ask too much of me. Come out into the sunlight."

"To be shot by your friends?"

"You are my friend. Come out and bind my ankles, if you think I shall run away. I was frightened by the rope round my neck. I will not run away again. But you must bind my ankles if you do not believe me. You are afraid of being shot?"

There was scorn in her voice.

She said coldly, "Use my body as a shield, so that if there is a bullet it will hit me and not you. The great Feringhia, your ancestor, would have laughed to see a Jemadar sheltering behind the body of a woman he says he loves, but if you are frightened of a little gun at a great distance that is what you must do."

Feringhia came out of the temple. He blinked for a moment in the full glare of the sun. He said mildly, "There is a difference between cowardice and caution."

"Yes. I do not think you are afraid. It is I who

am afraid. I am torn in two halves. I do not trust myself not to run away again. My mind will tell me to stay but my legs will run."

"Then I must tie your legs."

"Yes. You must tie them."

One of the brothers murmured, "This is not a trick. This cannot be a trick."

Feringhia took out his ruhmal of yellow and white cotton. He walked towards Veena. She came a few paces closer to the temple. Her head was meekly lowered.

Feringhia might not be frightened of the Europeans' guns, but he kept Veena between himself and them.

Feringhia crouched at Veena's feet in order to tie her ankles with the ruhmal. The brothers understood that this was a sure symbol that she would never again escape.

Veena leaned forward. The hem of her shawl touched Feringhia's shoulder. Suddenly she exclaimed and pointed.

A dozen of the brothers saw the small black lizard run down the back of Feringhia's cotton shirt.

There was a low, wailing chorus of utter dismay.

Feringhia turned, dropping the half-tied ruhmal. He said sharply, "What is it? What have you seen?"

They told him about the omen.

He turned angrily to Veena.

Veena had taken a few paces backwards. She held the ruhmal. There was something in her right hand under the ruhmal.

She said, "I saw it. It came suddenly, from nowhere, out of empty air. The most evil of omens. There is a curse on this shikar."

There was a murmur of agreement from the temple, a rustle of uneasy movement.

Feringhia shouted, "Woman of lies, you dropped the lizard! It is a false omen!"

"You may deceive yourself," said Veena. "You may deceive your brothers. But you will not deceive Kali. See. She looks at you now. Each snake of her girdle, each skull of her necklace watches you."

The brothers looked and gasped. It was true. The snakes of the girdle seemed to writhe and the skulls of the necklace to grin and the goddess herself to glare with fierce suspicion at Feringhia.

Veena said, "I do not know what will come to you if you ignore the omen of the lizard. But I think you know what will come to you, and I think your brothers know what will come to them. Is it a quick death or a slow one, or merely mutilation, or disgrace, or deaths among your children, or a plague among your cows?"

The brothers knew that their heads would stare backwards between their shoulder-blades, and perhaps their knees hinge backwards like those of their disjointed victims. They clamoured to Feringhia to leave at once.

"We will leave," said Feringhia to Veena. "But you will come with us."

"No."

"You will come with me, and for ever."

"No. I bring you ill fortune. I bring disaster to you and all your brothers. A turban fell onto the cooking fire while I was in your village. As long as I am there turbans will fall on fires and lizards on garments."

In spite of this threat, Feringhia rushed towards the girl. She whipped aside the ruhmal and revealed a pistol in her right hand. She fired it. She shot Feringhia in the hip. He spun from the impact of the bullet on his pelvis and crashed to the ground. He sobbed

with the pain, his big handsome face contorted under
the mane of silver hair.

There was simply an exodus. Little dark men, in
dhotis and pyjamas and flapping cotton shirts, slipped
out of the temple and away.

A party of four, the ones best known to Veena
when she was Veena, came quickly out of the temple
towards her. She backed away, holding the gun. Ig-
noring her, they picked up their Jemadar. He groaned
and fainted. They carried him, four men between
them, out of the portico.

Another party carried away the body of the fat
little guide.

The temple was deserted except for the two Europeans and one girl in a torn sari.

Sandro and Colly had not dared to move, in case
they broke the spell woven by Jenny and by her
lizard. Now they ran to her.

Jenny suddenly sat down on the rock floor of the
cavern. Her hands were trembling. With difficulty
she handed Colly's gun back to him.

She said shakily, "I wonder where the lizard went.
I'd like to keep him as a pet."

"And call him Ishur Ghose," suggested Colly.

"Ah," said Sandro. "Now we must make another
shikar."

When she said she was ready they pulled Jenny to
her feet. They went to the portico and very carefully
through it, guns concealed but ready. The track and
hillside were deserted. The army of Thugs had de-
materialised: evaporated into the escarpment of the
great green plain: become dozens of unconnected,
anonymous, humble, respectable individuals making
inconspicuous journeys in the cheapest ways.

Other tourists, unaccountably prevented from entering the temple, now trickled towards it. The chief guide, chins awag, was crying angrily for a man named Purohit. Eyebrows were raised at the sight of a beautiful but ragged Indian girl in the company of two opulent Europeans with a big car.

Sandro drove back towards Aurangabad.

Jenny said suddenly, "I hated shooting him. His mother is sweet."

The police had had no communication of any kind from anybody called Ishur Ghose. Near-certainty thus became certainty.

Colly agreed. "That way we maybe have a little more of a dossier. They may believe us. I doubt it, but they may."

They got European clothes for Jenny, a shirt and cotton pants. She felt strange in them. She took out the contact lenses, but she could do nothing about the colour of her skin or hair. The cornflower blue eyes in the dark face were even more startling than Sandro's.

They travelled, quickly and comfortably, 900 miles north-east; they went all three to Ishur Ghose's hotel.

They were met by lamentation.

Ishur Ghose had received a message. It caused him, although he was a freethinker, to announce that he was going into Benares to purify himself in the Ganges.

His body, drowned, had been recovered at a small ghat a little below the city.

His library included the literature of Thuggee— Sir William Sleeman's official reports and his dictionary of Ramasi, his grandson's definitive history, Hutton's *Popular Account,* the fictional *Confessions.* The books had been used, but no more than other books; they had not been annotated or marked in any way. They were books to be expected in any good library of Indian history. The police found nothing incriminating among Ishur Ghose's effects; they were not able to trace any relevant contact.

Kashi's yellow and white cotton scarf was examined by a museum curator. Jenny's account of the murder of the Ellora guide was typed and circulated. Her scrappy memories were checked against Sleeman's voluminous reports.

"My God," said Colly. "On that train I happened to be a sitar player. That's why I didn't get rubbed."

Official incredulity broke down. Slowly, reluctantly, belief grew. Tight security was kept, as far as tight security was possible in India.

The disappearances did not cease, but they almost did. Only five were reported in a month.

But the Thugs were not dead until they were dead.

The task of the police was a good deal easier than Sleeman's had been in 1829. They knew a great deal more. Their communications were much better. They were alerted to the infiltration of their own ranks. There were no deviously-managed native states where the government's writ did not run, no permanent boltholes, no high-ranking protection. It was easier but it was not easy. It was not quick. It was unlikely to be truly comprehensive. The problem surely existed in Pakistan; it might there be identified and contained. It undoubtedly existed in Bangla Desh; in the famine, disorder, poverty and profiteering of that unfortunate country the problem had probably not even been noticed amidst the cheapness of human lives and the misery and the mess.

Kashi's village was with great difficulty identified.

Kashi was found with a splintered pelvis. He did not talk but others did. They showed fear of imprisonment, torture, execution, but they showed no remorse, no trace of repugnance.

Jenny's evidence convicted Kashi and several of his friends of murder or of being accessory to murder. After interminable identity parades, Colly was able to testify about the murders on the train and the attempted murder in the Pilgrim House. But—as in the 1830s—the police relied for the great bulk of their case on confessions and on the exposure of one Thug by another. It had been surprising to Sleeman that the brothers should so readily betray each other; it was surprising still.

"I guess," said Colly, "it's because they don't think they have anything to be ashamed of."

Two hundred and three bodies were found, not one of which would ever have been found without either the confession of a Thug or the betrayal of one by another. All the bodies were gashed and disjointed; every grave was totally, perfectly camouflaged.

Three hundred and eleven persons were arrested, of whom all but sixty went on trial. In a lamentable number of cases the evidence did not justify conviction on a charge of murder, but only on such lesser charges as conspiracy, theft, or harbouring fugitives from justice.

Publicity, though not prevented, was discouraged. The government, intermittently sensitive to Western opinion, did not want too much talk about the ancient savageries of a half-civilised society; nobody wanted panic; nobody wanted reprisals, or the cynical excuse for reprisals of the kind with which Parisian businessmen liquidated their rivals after the Liberation. The crimes were always referred to as murder or robbery; Thuggee was mentioned seldom and deprecatingly.

A large part of India saw the whole thing as a communist plot; another large part as a C.I.A. plot; hippies were also blamed.

Kashi, Sanghavi, Lal Chand and a hundred others got life imprisonment.

There was insufficient evidence to bring Muni to trial. Jenny was relieved. She did not want to give evidence against Muni.

"I don't see why," said Colly. "*She* doesn't think *she* has anything to be ashamed of."

Nor did she. Nor did any of the women, the young children, the older men who had escaped detection, or the survivors of the brotherhood who lay in hiding.

They knew that the sect could never be altogether killed. There need was only one pregnant woman of their number, one man-child. In time all would start again as it had been. Ruhmal the strangling scarf would be rewoven, Kussi the sacred pickaxe unburied.

There were seven disappearances in the next month.

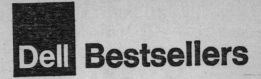

Dell Bestsellers

At your local bookstore or use this handy coupon for ordering: